A Kiss for the Cursed

DANIEL CARLSON

Chapter 1

"Load up the bag!" the Outlaw ordered, pointing his fabled Tranter revolver through the iron bars at Dick Bewley, the cashier at Barton's Bank, Dry Springs, Gonzales County, Texas, and thrust a compressed bag between the bars.

"What?" Dick spat with a high-pitched startle, realising his recurring nightmares had been a warning premonition.

He knew deep inside that today was going to be a bad day. A superstitious man, Dick's life was regulated by strict routine, and any deviation from his habitual practices always seemed to result in unwelcomed consequences.

Today he feared the worst when he arose to find his housekeeper had substituted his usual hard-boiled breakfast egg with a lard roll.

"You heard me."

The Outlaw raised his brow at the suddenly pallid face beyond the steel bars. "Fill the bag."

The command was calm and controlled, the tone threatening and absolute, the pistol levelled firm and precise. Dick's eyes flicked between the half-cast smile of the robber and Mrs Webb, the bank's only customer, who stood rigid with her back pressed against the wall and her arms bolt aloft.

He wiped the instantly forming beads of sweat from his forehead and ruffled the fringe on his immaculately greased hair as he saw Webb begin to mutter silent prayers.

"What you waiting for?"

Dick's hands trembled on a pile of documents to his front.

"What's going on Mr B…ew…ley?" stuttered Talbot Jennings, the bank manager, as his round face appeared at the side of his understudy.

"Oh, my God." he mouthed, instantly recognising the unsheathed face of the infamous Outlaw from the wanted posters.

Jennings's eyes bulged and his usual rosy face blanched, realising his life was in peril. He took one extraordinarily long blink, wishing he had kissed his wife before leaving for work instead of rushing out late for work as always.

Steel against steel clanked as the Outlaw tapped the barrel of the Tranter against the protective railings and jolted Jennings out of his lament.

"Give me all you've got and be quick about it." he ordered.

"We haven't got a lot with the war en all. Cash is …"

Thunder and smoke bellowed from the pistol and the clock at the rear of the two officials exploded into fragments, with shards of glass and wood splinters covering the cowering men.

"I didn't ask you how much you've got. I said give me everything you've got." He flicked a glance behind him.

"Seems to me folks around here are a little hard of understanding."

He smiled at Webb, who returned a jaw-sagged gasp as now she too recognised the face of Texas's most wanted man.

The Tranter roared another blast into the ceiling and white flurries dropped onto the heads and shoulders of the two animated men.

"And be quick about it."

Being well versed on the exploits of the Outlaw, the banker knew death would be administered swiftly if he defied or procrastinated, and so he grabbed the old corn sack with his shaking fingers and, sliding it across the counter, he spun to face the shiny black safe.

"Sheriff Al will have heard those shots."

Jennings could not hear his own words, his ears pained with the roar from the Outlaw's blast.

"And if you don't get to filling that bag, he'll hear another one soon enough."

Jennings lip-read the unfearing riposte.

"Ain't nobody got nothing anymore in these parts." the bank manager continued to mutter as the key clanked in the huge lock.

"Everybody's broke and ruined due to this god darn war. Ain't a spare nickel anywhere."

The solid iron door swung outwards and, angling his head, the Outlaw glimpsed the scant pile of notes in the dark cavity before Bewley's skinny frame blocked the view as he knelt to assist his quivering superior.

"Quit your wailing and fill the bag." the Outlaw ordered as the high midday sun beamed its orange cast through the high windows and sprayed its glow across the Outlaw, the counter, and the backs of the kneeling bankers.

"There'll be no place in the house of the Lord for your kind." Jennings continued his mutterings.

"Can't say I'd be welcomed a place anywhere."

Splashing water irritated the Outlaw's ears, and he slanted his head in the direction of the splattering to notice Mrs Webb's nerves had defied her and urine pooled around her feet. Turning his smile back towards Jennings and ensuring no one was foolhardy enough to show any signs of ignorant courage, he demanded,

"What's taking so long?"

"Been as q...q...q...quick as ... I... I... I... could." Jennings stuttered, and spinning, he held out in front of him the loose sack. "All ...we ... g...g...g...got." He slid the bag easily under the bars. "Ever...r...r...r...y darn c...c...c.c...cent."

Holding firm the pistol, the Outlaw grabbed the bag with his left hand and felt the weightlessness.

"Times sure are hard. Maybe it's time I found an alternative profession."

He shook the bag a couple more times, then he shook his head.

"You folks in these parts sure are having it tough. Ain't no point in going out into the desert to bury this."

Fearful of the robber's intentions, both of the men and the woman remained silent, standing almost perfectly still with nervous twitches displaying their distress.

"Well, you make sure you tell the press boys that I was all nice and polite now." He slipped his finger from the hammer and holstered the Tranter.

"Don't want any more of that melodramatic falsifying."

Without feeling the need to rush, he moved towards the door and tipped the brim of his hat.

"Ma'am." he addressed the woman with a brash smile, which confirmed her suspicions.

His pure grey eyes and perfectly aligned pearly teeth surpassed all the legendary and previously considered exaggerated reports of the fiercely handsome, but hated, Outlaw.

With the money bag gripped tightly, he flipped the closed sign which he had only minutes earlier turned, and the chimes from the doorbell confirmed his exit.

Stepping out into the brilliance, he squinted in both directions of the dusty street. Nothing interested him.

The boardwalks lay deserted and stillness loomed over the silent town. Only a barking hound in the distance broke the faint howling of intermittent gusts, which raised and dropped clouds of dust in its aftermath.

He had witnessed this false serenity many times before.

Beyond the peace and calm, net curtains twitched, shutters creaked, and doors were kept ajar, still he knew the sound of gunfire was the call to death for the plucky fools who would try to stand in his way.

Like most towns embroiled with the split of loyalties, the Civil War had already attracted the brave and he knew this time his shots in the bank would only rouse the curiosity of the peering cowards, the reckless fame grabbers, and the naive glory hunters.

Again he glanced in both directions, pulling down his brim to shield his eyes from the midday sun which bore down unfiltered from high above the clear blue. Across the street, a pure white Arabian at the hitch rail outside the El Toro Saloon caught his eye.Distinct in its poise, head held high, the Arabian stood out from its three companions, a chestnut Sorrel and two Morgans.

The Outlaw idled momentarily as he studied the horse and its equally magnificent tack, his hand hovering above the walnut handle of the Tranter, a cautionary action on the off chance someone from the saloon had the audacity or tequila-plied courage borne from ignorance to try and retrieve the town's measly wealth.

He speculated for the briefest of moments, glancing in the shadows that a shooter may be taking aim. Undeterred, he casually continued to tread the planks which led the way to his horse.

He did not respect life, death did not control his fears or tame his appetite for taking risks. He valued nothing and nothing excited him, to him death was inconsequential and eventually it comes to all. This world offered nothing to caution his disregard for seeing the next sunrise, he loved no one and no one loved him.

Untethering his horse, he was aware of the creaking wood behind him before the order was hollered.

"Get your hands up high where I can see them." The order was delivered with an evenly pitched drawl.

He obliged the call and turned his neck.

"Don't move!"

"Ain't a man got a right to face his maker?" He ignored the command.

"Not in my town. Now stay put or I'll fill you full of lead."

"Sheriff eh?" Looking over his shoulder, the Outlaw could not see the glistening pin which was proudly displayed.

"That's right. Sheriff Al Parker, and I'm taking you in." He exclaimed loud enough for the town's peepers to hear. "You've fired your last shot and robbed your last bank, Outlaw!" He boasted, his face mottled with both fear and rage.

"You don't sound so sure, sheriff." The Outlaw challenged. "Is that a jittery quiver of fear I hear in your voice?" He provoked.

"Just quit your rabbiting and drop the belt."

"As you say, sheriff."

"And hurry up about it." The sheriff took one step closer to sure up his aim. "We've had too many of your kind passing through this way and I'm going to send a warning message to 'em all."

"I doubt it." The Outlaw knew he was one of a kind. There were no resemblances close to compare.

"Folks don't take too kindly to you helping yourself to their wares." The sheriff continued to inch forward whilst holding tight his aim. "It's gonna be mightily pleasing to swing you from that old tree you see down yonder."

Assured invincibility and eternal certainty pulsed through the Outlaw's veins, just as it always did when he was challenged by a lesser being.

"Don't rightly think so, sheriff." He stretched his fingers. "Pine or oak?"

"What?" The sheriff scowled.

"Coffin, do you want pine or oak?"

By the time the words had reached the sheriff, the Outlaw had spun and withdrawn his revolver.

Sheriff Parker momentarily hesitated as he absorbed the piercing grey eyes of the man five yards away, his body locked rigid with a terror he had not encountered before. His forehead rutted and his eyes widened as he realised he was not just face to face with a robber, but the notorious outlaw whose sketched portrait had been displayed on the 'dead or alive' board for the last seven years.

Finally, he squeezed hard on the trigger of his Colt.

Two explosions bellowed and the thud of lead piercing through flesh and bone was heard as the sheriff crashed to the floor with a newly acquired hole in his face. In the same instant, the Outlaw's horse screamed, reared up, and pulled away from the hitch rail as lead from the sheriff's wayward bullet stung deep into its hindquarters.

Blood spouted waist high from the dead sheriff's face and dripped heavily from the bolting horse, which was disappearing down the deserted street.

The Outlaw swiftly spun, directing his pistol towards doorways, windows, street corners, and rooftops.

He sensed only inquisitive and cowardly gazes and he sighed with disappointment when there were no more unwise lawmen or heroes stepping out from the dark or aiming weapons from behind protective barriers.

He smiled and casually slid his renowned life taker back into its leather at the side of his hip.

Nonchalance continued to crease his cheeks as he cast one final glance at the blood-covered prostrate figure and wondered what remarks the dailys would print in tomorrow's headlines.

With his horse injured and scampering out of sight, he crossed the wide dirt street to approach the four horses strapped outside El Toro.

He paused only for the briefest of moments as his attention again searched for signs of danger from the darkness behind the saloon's swinging panelled doors, then he turned his focus to the mighty Arabian by his side. Without further delay, he unstrapped the thoroughbred and swung himself into the decorated polished saddle.

Peering out from behind the saloon door, Judge Bechstein, whose regular Monday afternoon poker had been ruined by the shots and the murder on the street, cussed repeatedly as he watched the killer gallop away into the sun-blazed distance on his most prized possession.

From his top pocket, he pulled out a crisp handkerchief to dap his sweat-damped forehead, then, stroking his enormous white walrus moustache, he bellowed,

"Send me a wire to Austin. I want a posse and I want one now!"

Chapter 2

The citizens of Rio Rojo were an inhospitable assembly of embittered and untrusting souls who, due to the misery of the Civil War, had learned to live and survive from the barest scraps of life's pleasures.

The friendless town, consisting of small scattered mainly single-storey white stone and wooden dwellings, was situated between Austin and Abilene. Surrounded by a barren landscape, which was mostly void of any natural resources, a vastness of wild grass overran the landscape on one side of the town and hard wind-swept soil spread as far as the eye could see in the opposite direction.

A couple of ranchers struggled to survive and trade, but mainly the town prospered by just being a stopover for travellers and cattlemen. The single wide street of mainly farming merchandise stores and provisions was named Red Water by the original Mexican settlers whose brief stay was ended by the arrival of Sam Houston many years later.

Before the ravaging war years, the town prospered. Surrounded by fertile cattle land, trading was brisk and opportunities for business thrived, however the town had been pillaged many times by both the armies of the North and South who had left the county exhausted of materials, stocks, and exempt from wealth.

At first, the townsfolk rallied to offer support for their brothers of the South. Eager and willing, they donated as much food and supplies as they could to strengthen the assailing army, however in the following months, defeated and distressed retreating soldiers in grey plundered whatever they could carry as they fled with panic from the advancing merciless blue bellies.

Conditions worsened and resentment set in as the advancing and trespassing army of the North stole or destroyed anything of value. Homes were stripped, larders emptied, and work equipment damaged to prevent any type of Southern prosperity. Most men fled, leaving their wives and daughters to defend themselves or plea for mercy from the devilish northern monsters whose immoral behaviour was beyond all control.

Now, the blues had been forced back by the resurgent Confederate army, but the returning menfolk had as yet been unable to re-establish any kind of prosperous normality to the region. Businesses and households had been left with scarce commodities, livestock, or supplies for themselves and they had to be selfish to ensure their own self-preservation and endurance. They had become mean and resentful to all and they had no sympathy for the needy, weak, or infrequent saddle-weary travellers. Most had aged and become embittered and disenchanted by the fighting, their lives felt meaningless and they held no remorse for the dead of both the blue and grey.

The town was unusual from its neighbouring pueblos due to it being almost as quiet by day as it was by night.

The tranquillity was not a deception. Come dusk, the saloons, gambling houses, and dens of inequity all remained bare of buoyant gun-wielding and cash-burdened revellers because most of Rio Rojo's fit men enlisted in the fight at the first opportunity. The others who chose to stay out of the conflict soon fled when the distant rumbles of the blue invaders grew to within earshot and so all that was left to occupy the poker tables were the old, weak, and the ruling militia which had returned to menace the few who had decided to persevere with their obligations in Rio Rojo.

Windswept soil lay thick on the untrodden boardwalks that bordered the wide, expansive street. Doors were spragged open to circulate the late summer's slight breeze and although most of the storerooms were empty and only dust occupied the shelves, the proprietors hoped to entice passing amblers to venture inside to part with some much-needed greenbacks.

To the north end of Main Street, situated on a rise and positioned on the entrance to the town, stood a stone-built church with a bell tower which could be seen above a nestle of Spanish red oaks for miles around. The imposing building stood proud on the edge of town as if it had been built to strategically watch over the town's evildoers and act as God's witness for Judgment Day.

It was here, within a small tended and vegetated enclosure and amongst the carefully arranged grave markers and remembrance carvings in the kingdom of the dead, that the preacher hung a dead list every Sunday before service.

Tearful eyes would dreadfully linger over the paper, which coldly bore the souls of men who had gone to fight for their beliefs against the northern oppressors and were destined never to return.

In contrast to the serenity of the peace garden, at the opposite end of the town grew a magnificent cedar, which was known to the locals as the hanging tree. From here, the villains who met their death at the end of a rope were not privileged to be planted in the tended and blessed garden of the Lord, instead their lifeless entities sunk into the barren slope on a far hill where only a stone marked their presence.

The cedar served Rio Rojo well and the assembly of carefully placed stones bore testament to its value. Facing the hanging tree was Sheriff Gisty's office. A single wooden fortress which only stood out from the other buildings because of the wide planking which had been designed to permit inquisitors to study the descriptions and likenesses of the lawless wanted.

Weekly the notices were updated, new rewards offered, and the captured or dead removed, however one poster remained, only being replaced by a newer version as the prominently positioned print became faded and tattered.

The character exhibited with the highest reward money ever offered, dead or alive, was a man with no name who had blighted the state with his villainous adventures for the last five years.

Identified to the curious and to the many pursuers only as the Outlaw, little truth was known about the medium-framed man with blonde wavy hair, ghostly grey eyes, and sun-stained skin, yet everyone knew all there was to know about the killer.

Legendary fables of his exploits were exaggerated throughout the schoolyards and saloons alike. His devilment and daring audacity was revered by the young and naive. Tongues spread hushed admiration throughout the haberdasheries and mercantiles for his prose and appeal. His yellow hair shone like a crown and his steel grey eyes were known to enchant women into trances of unspeakable desires. His draw was as quick as lightning and his aim was deathly sure. He had hurled forty men into eternity and robbed every bank north of San Antonio, yet he only killed Yankee men and robbed Yankee banks. He was a cavalier who only stole to fund the rebels, he was a Confederate General frustrated by the failings of bureaucracy, he was a minister ordained by God to rid the world of wrongdoers, malcontents, and traitors. Boys acted out his daring feats of bravery, girls fantasised about being saved from Indians by him.

Shopkeepers, gamblers, bank owners, and lawmen all feared him and stayed clear of reported sightings and bounty hunters unwisely gave up their lives increasingly. Fables, exaggerations, and the truth spread daily, yet to the public he was a mystery, a ghost, a hero, and a villain. He was seen in every county, yet tracking him seemed impossible.

Reports from the lawmen were few, but his exploits were printed daily on every broadsheet. He was not afraid to face a smoking gun, and he delivered death daily. He was an exhibitionist who flaunted himself in society and teased the regulators. He was the people's bandit and he was a true Christian sent to steal from the sinful and give to the poor.

All of which was mainly untrue, and the truth was lame and dull in comparison. Only he, the Outlaw, knew the truth of his beginnings, his principles, and exactly how many men he had exterminated in cold-blooded murder and only he knew how many sleepy towns had been left short of funds due to his thievery. He was the only one that knew his age, his motivation, and his name, to the rest he was an enigma whom they called 'The Outlaw'.

Chapter 3

Dust rose from the lone rider in the distance. A dark silhouette against a sinking huge orange ball, the horseman approached Rio Rojo with a leisurely trot.

The dozen or so babblers who stalked the boardwalks squinted westwards at the cloud of dust half a mile distant.

Visitors passing through Rio Rojo, especially lone riders, had become rare since the nation's conflict had descended upon the county and the stir of dust began to provoke a rare excitement.

The town gave no one a reason to visit, there was little attraction other than to rest up before moving on quickly, so the speculating townsfolk squinted hard and shielded their eyes as they pondered with interest the stranger's approach.

Only slanting a curious glance as he passed the white church, the rider paraded down the wide main street unconcerned by what reception lay ahead.

"It's him." murmured a parasol-holding woman to his left.

"It can't be."

He ignored the whispers.

"It is …. It's definitely him."

"You sure?"

"Sure as I'm standing here …… who else rides a horse like that?"

"Looks like Judge Beckstein's ride to me?"

The Outlaw kept his eyes fixed straight.

"You mean the old judge over in Dry Springs?"

"There's only one Arabian like that within two hundred miles of here." exclaimed an old-timer walking up close to the two women.

"The devil himself … all dandy on the judge's horse en all." chastised a third woman who joined the group.

"The audacity." grumbled the old-timer, clamping on his pipe.

The mutterings fell silent, and only scampering steps could be heard as the onlookers scurried into their safe havens. Shutters creaked and nets ruffled as tongues quickly spread the news of the Outlaw's arrival.

Riding tall on the pure white Arabian, the Outlaw's eyes remained fixed ahead. He lipped the sign above the double doors, 'Eduardo's Barra de Tequila', all the time noting the peers and gazes at every doorway and window.

The reason for his visit to town was now in front of him, no more than ten paces away. He licked his lips and tasted dust and sweat. He had a desert thirst that needed quenching and a grumbling gut that needed filling and he was intent on satisfaction.

Fearing no cowardly shots from out of the shadows, he continued the slow pace until he reached the destination rail.

He swung down from the leather-creaking saddle and patted the solid hind of the Arabian, then he glided his hand across the ornately etched saddle.

After quickly inspecting his roll and duster, which he had acquired from his own horse whilst it grazed in a thicket a few miles outside Dry Springs, he hitched his new ride alongside two nags.

Leather treading the wooden steps announced his arrival at the spragged-open door of the cantina.

He paused before entering the darkness, not out of concern or fear. He was angst-ridden by his weather-battered appearance. In the doorway a cloud lifted as he patted off the dust of travel from his lavish tailored outfit.

Noted for his flamboyancy, which the ordinary hardworking could not afford, today the Outlaw's attire surpassed all previous exaggerations. His leg-hugging denims, which displayed a seam of copper studs down the outer side, were matched in exuberance by a black French placket shirt which was adorned by a grey and green paisley decoration. Around his chest and back, a perfectly fitting leather vest was detailed with elaborate stampings. Completing the outfit was a newly acquired black Vaquero hat and a highly waxed, large-buckled Concho belt which seated his Tranter pistol.

The silence within the gloomy fetid bar room was only broken by the creaking of a closing door toward the rear. The Outlaw's eyes, accustomed from the brightness, adjusted as the darkness cleared and he scanned across the deserted tables and bar.

Chairs and stools were scattered. The poker table displayed cards, coins, and drinks which had been abandoned in haste and without any thoughts of conclusion.

Smoke from a half-chewed cigarillo rose directly from the snuff box where it had hastily been discarded next to half-filled shot glasses.

The Outlaw walked across the sawdust, spilled beer, and spit to drag a stool to the bar. Stretching out his bones, he had second thoughts about reseating himself after just completing a long dry ride. He rested his foot on a makeshift foot rail and arched over the bar to grab the nearest bottle of spirit, then, knocking off the seal on the bar top, he swigged a large mouthful of the poison.

As the liquor stung his dry throat he frowned upon the bottle label, 'Viva Tequila', then he glanced across at the discarded cards and smiled at the sight of the probable winning hand, a straight flush, all spades.

His eyes returned to the front where opposite him hung the largest mirror he had ever seen.

The huge glass rectangle was surrounded by a thick decorated walnut frame which boasted two small oval inset mirrors at each end.

He studied his appearance and ran his hand through his flattened blonde greasy weave, then he scratched his three-day stubble. He sighed at the travel-tired and weather-beaten reflection which aged him and he replaced his vaquero to cover the dull locks.

Rising smoke behind him caught his attention in the glass and he swivelled at the waist to look again towards the gambling table. He hauled himself upright and casually ambled towards the discarded play. He lifted the burning cigarillo to his lips and inhaled a lungful of smoke until the relaxing sensation turned into an irritation that caused him to cough repeatedly.

He briefly studied the cards. Either side of the straight flush were discarded plays and a large kitty centred the round table. He looked at the remaining unplayed hand and raised the corner of one card, then he used the corner of the card to flip over, one at a time, the remaining four cards. A smile cut through his curiosity. 'I win,' he mused as he tossed over an ace, queen, king and a jack to complete a royal flush.

He removed his hat, sliding the plunder across the table and into the felt crown, then with the cigar in hand he returned to the bottle he left on the bar.

His mood was sullen, and he was morose.

Over the past few months, he had grown disenchanted with his occupation as slowly, day by day, he began to lose the thrill and satisfaction he gained from inflicting pain and suffering upon those who dared to stand in his way.

No longer did a pulse rush through his veins as he taunted death's passage. Disappearing fast was his dauntless lust for life.

During the many lonely nights under the stars, his recollections of daring exploits and his grandiose self-esteem were slowly being alienated by dour reminiscences as the pained and horrified faces of his victims haunted his dreams and illusory torturous images of their suffering loved ones, whose lives had been shattered by his nonchalant approach to God's true gift, implanted themselves on the back of his eyelids.

Life no longer appealed to him as it once did. All he found appealing now was the thought of an endless sleep.

He had noticed over the past few months his considerations for his actions and his blindness to the consequences were gradually being turned into a never-experienced-before dullness of regret which loomed heavily on his thoughts.

He had not deliberately chosen this profession, neighbouring family squabbles at a young age turned into feuds followed by violence which led him onto a path of no return and onto the trail of death.

At first, his own self-preservation and survival commanded him until wanton, unmerciful brutality became the rule. By the time he was fifteen, both his brothers and his father had been killed by local adversaries in the dispute that riled the entire nation and, without the restraining presence of his father, coldness developed and his conscience ebbed into nonexistence.

He gulped again from the bottle, the bitterness and burn failed to exterminate the cloudy melancholy of self-pity. He took another dose of the medicine, this time the venomous liquid seemed to have lost its throat-scraping potency and he swigged again and again, only occasionally stopping to draw tobacco smoke.

Hurriedly approaching footsteps from outside stirred his attention, but not enough for him to draw his weapon to protect himself. Instead, he casually leant on the bar gazing into the mirror ready to accept his fate.

The ceramic spittoon beneath his feet hissed as he tossed the exhausted cigar to watch in the mirror a shadow glide past the saloon window to his rear, then the noise of heels on wood increased as someone approached the door.

Still, he gave no thought to caution and his fingers remained wrapped around the bottle. His passion for life was exhausted, and he cared little for his prospects. A bullet in the back of his head was his desire, yet he feared the noose neither, and he remained unconcerned by the approach. He was ready to accept his fate and God's will.

The door flung open and illumination dazzled, still his inquisitiveness was not drawn and he lowered his eyes from the flash of blaze in the mirror. His hand tensed around the bottle and he prepared to take his last swig.

"Find my son!" exclaimed the dark figure in the doorway.

The Outlaw gulped down the mouthful of liquor and frowned as the words, and not the thunderous blast as he expected, reached his ears. The call intrigued him and he curiously raised his eyes towards the mirror.

"Please find my son."

Behind him stood a silhouette of a woman, her features hidden with a hood and the intensity of the surrounding orange from beyond the open door.

"What?" he heard her call and muttered with disbelief as he failed to comprehend the meaning.

"Find my son." The woman closed the door behind her, blocking out the setting sun.

"I heard." he said.

"I want you to find my son." she cried.

The Outlaw remained unmoved, his eyes unravelling her emerging appearance. A pained, but determined stern grimace screened her desperation, and she gave no consideration to the danger she put herself in by approaching the devil.

Again he heard her words and again he failed to understand her demand. He remained silent, allowing his eyes to follow her as, without fear or hesitation, she marched to his side.

He couldn't remember anyone approaching him before unless they had a pistol drawn ready to kill and, stunned, he leant back slightly as her undaunted advance intrigued him.

She opened a homemade carpet valise, and he watched without reaction expecting her to withdraw a weapon, instead a confused frown appeared on his face as she pulled out a bulging canvas bag which clanked as she dropped it on the bar in front of him. Then she fidgeted in the bag once more to produce a tin plate which this time she placed carefully in front of his eyes. Carefully she removed her hood in the hazy light and he noticed the welling in her reddened and tired eyes.

"I want…" Tears flowed. "I need you to find my son." she gasped with a tremor of anguish.

His eyes flicked between the purse, the picture of a boy and her teary face.

Bob Darell was etched on the tin plate beneath the portrait of a young man.

"Uh." He couldn't find any words and he clamped hard his teeth, expecting to hear the bellowed wrath of a young widow's fury.

"Instead of taking lives, I want you to save one." she spat.

"I'm not in that line of business, ma'am." he replied quickly with a scowl.

"I'm willing to pay." She slid the bag nearer to him and tugged the cord to expose the haul of coins and notes. "And good too. It's everything I've got."

"I'm not interested."

"It's not Yankee money." She tried to appeal to his rumoured Southern principles.

"You've got the wrong man." His tone was sure, confirming he was not interested.

"Man? ……. men uh. As you will have noticed around these parts my options are limited." She continued undeterred, referring to the lack of able men. "From what I've heard."

"You're not listening." he cut in. "I'm not interested." he dismissed. "Take your money and leave."

"Have you never lost a loved one or known grief?" It was a statement, not a question.

"What?" He subconsciously shook his head slightly, not in response to her remark, he was still shocked by her approach.

"I can tell you, mister, that a mother's love is unconditional and only deep pain stands as witness to the love which has passed." With shaking fingers, she removed a handkerchief.

"I'm not the angel you're looking for."

He slanted his eyes to watch her dab the flow of tears from her cheek, but he was unmoved. He did not care where her son was or what trouble he was in.

"Not looking for an angel." She moved her face closer to him and stared into his light eyes which contrasted vividly against the colouration of his face. "An angel will take my boy away for good, not bring him home."

He could feel the warmth of her breath, he could smell the subtle freshness of cleanliness as she continued undeterred.

"You've got a fanciful imagination."

"I know what I'm looking for and it sure ain't an angel." She searched for a flicker of compassion in those famed cold grey eyes. "Far from it."

There was no trace of pity or empathy. "It is more the devil himself I'm looking for. Only a demon can get me my son back."

"Well, that maybe I am, but being your boy's saviour interests me none."

He raised the bottle to his lips and drank then groaned. "Even with all your coins, I'm not the shining light you're looking for. I'm sorry."

He stopped speaking, he felt awkward, he had never apologised to anyone before and it felt strange.

"I'm begging you." Again she tried to stem the flow of tears with the embroidered cloth. "My love for my son has become a curse. My boy needs help and I need you."

"I can't help you. You see my time treading on earth's dirt is through." He lowered his head. "And I'm just waiting to meet my maker so I can start my journey into the inferno of hell. No amount of money is going to turn me now and put me on the path of the righteous."

"Well, maybe you could turn for God. Turn his judgement upon you with one final passing." She would not relent.

"I'm not for turning and neither is my God. My mind is set. I'm just waiting to feel the cloak of death wrap upon my soul. You'll have to find another man, a man more righteous and divine ……. a man that's hungry for money." He was cold to her despair.

"It's not a righteous or hungry man I need. As I said, it's a devil. Only a demon will be able to reach into the claws of death and pull out my son alive." This time exasperation replaced her vulnerable tones.

"Your wallowing changes nothing. It's as I said. I'm just passing through this way and soon the world will be a better place without the likes of men like me."

She reacted by reaching out and lifting the bottle from his grip to take a long swig from the neck. The burn rasped her throat and coarsened her voice.

"I'm begging you. Please consider my plea."

He didn't reply, instead he grasped the bottle back from her and raised it to his lips.

"Every day that he is in danger, my heart bleeds. The longing for him to return home never fades. The pain is raw." The breeze from her words could be felt on his cheeks.

"You ain't listening. I'm not that type of man."

Her appeal to a forgotten memory of sadness failed. "How do you live with the ghosts you have sent to the abyss?"

"I figure I'll be with them soon enough."

Desperate to ignite passion or sentiment, she persisted. "Are you the type of man that has never known love?"

"I've heard love makes you mad." He sneered.

"Well if love makes you mad then I am indeed mad and I will do anything …… anything to get my son back."

She did not wait for apathy nor an invitation to continue. She was distraught and desperate and she spoke from the heart without realising.

She explained in detail how her boy, who was just thirteen, had been bullied into enlisting by the rebel militia.

"He had been out playing with the other boys and as a dare, they sneaked into Macklin Buck's ranch to steal some eggs."

She continued at pace and without a pause for breath. "One of Mac's ranch hands caught the slower runners as they fled, one of them being Bobby Ray, my son."

Again the woman stretched out for the bottle and the Outlaw released his grip without any objection.

After another swig and wiping her lips, she continued.

"That no-good mean-spirited mongrel sent for the captain of the militia to administer whatever punishment they saw fit and without Bobby Ray's papa around to stand up and defend him against the militia he didn't stand a chance."

Her voice trembled, and this time she paused and hesitated.

"You see the militia run this county and with all the men gone away to fighting the Yankees they bully everyone and help themselves to anything and everything which is not offered, including young men and boys near to fighting age." She glanced over her shoulder towards the door. "Anyone who falls foul of their wicked ways is beaten and bundled off to the enlistment office in Austin, never to be seen or heard of again until their names appear on the dead list at the church gates.

They all know in these parts when they're sent off to fighting they must still obey and oblige the militia, or should I say Captain Tillman, because if they don't their loved ones who are left behind are subjected to the most horrendous and cruel treatment."

Although the Outlaw's face remained stoic he listened through her pain. He admitted inwardly that he would like to meet the coward, Captain Tillman, and look him in the eye.

"Sarah, young Todd's mama, who was with my Bobby, well she saw her son's name on the dead list last Sunday and she passed out right there and then outside the church. The poor woman's been bed-bound ever since and it's only a matter of time before she passes over taking with her those final few written words of young Todd's finality. 'Brave Todd Brewer killed in the battle of Poison Spring. Aged eighteen.'"

She released a long sigh and composed herself again.

"Only he wasn't, he wasn't brave and he wasn't eighteen. He was bullied into signing up just like my Bobby and he was only fifteen. Those boys can't look after themselves out there on the field of death, they can't even steal eggs for Christ's sake. They need saving."

Her voice rasped and her throat dried. "You know that the loss of a child is the greatest pain inflicted on the soul and it leaves scars so deep they never heal."

Her glazed eyes bore directly into the face of the Outlaw.

"That so. Well, I'm sorry for your troubles and for your boy." He was a veteran of cruelty and he remained unmoved by her touching appeal. "Nevertheless, it's as I said. I'm not your man."

"Yes, you are. You are that man. I know it and I can feel it inside. Any man who can clear a bar without even speaking a word is what I'm looking for." She levelled out her right arm and swung it across the scramble of empty chairs.

"Only a man with that mastery can go into the belly of the Yankees to pull my son out alive and bring him home."

Even before he replied she knew her plea had failed to appeal to his morals.

"You need an honest man, a preacher, an apostle or someone who can explain the futility of such a forlorn ambition. Not a man who cares little for life's privileges."

He knew many would take the woman's money, also he knew no one would engage in such a dangerous charter.

"Ain't you got any better suggestions?" She questioned his sanity.

"I'd say praying with the Bible would be better."

The intensity of his unmerciful dismissal mentally numbed her, and she turned away to wipe more tears. "You keep walking through uninviting doors and you'll soon be occupying a grave." She added, talking through the damp handkerchief.

"I figure," he slid the heavy bag of coins back in her direction. "Now take your money and leave me be." He grasped the bottle from in front of her. "No amount of cash will bring about my redemption."

"No, but saving the life of one of God's innocent children might." She replied.

"Doubt that. My ticket to the damned is already stamped."

He raised the bottle to his lips again and this time his drink lasted longer, then he slammed the bottle hard on the counter as he announced with finality.

"Now go and leave me be. Take your squawking and wallowing someplace else where you might find someone with a sympathetic ear."

Recognising his words were absolute and tired of beseeching for mercy and sympathy, she turned on her heels.

"Then I hope you enjoy your ride."

She had doubted that he had a conscience, still she was hurt that her initial suspicions had been proven correct.

"May your soul never find peace."

Nearing the door, anger and desolation began to set in, and knowing that she had failed to rouse any mercenary interest she abandoned hope. "Because neither will mine."

He caught her final sobbing words as she exited and he mused at her courage as he watched through the mirror her grieving, stooping body stagger away dejectedly with the dream and hopes of seeing her son alive crushed.

Leaving Eduardo's, the gathering at the doorway and on the boardwalks scrambled in all directions to avoid any contact with the Outlaw, and the street virtually abandoned within a few seconds.

Only one man remained, his silver badge reflecting on the Outlaw's face. The sheriff's stern countenance was shaded by his deliberately low-placed brim, yet it did not prevent the Outlaw from detecting aged skin around high cheekbones and a sagging under alert, but sullen eyes. Draping from beneath his hat and covering his ears was long hair streaked with a grey deterioration and although he looked ten years past his peak he was still a big, tall man.

The Outlaw knew this sheriff still demanded and got respect from the townspeople of Rio Rojo.

The sheriff brooded intensely at the Outlaw. Smoke whirled in front of his face from the stub of a chewed cigar. He had no time for outsiders, especially ones like the vermin that stood less than ten feet away.

All the life-threatening years of governing Rio Rojo had not sapped his vigour for keeping the peace and cold-blooded murderers turned the pit of his stomach.

The enforcer had been resting on the steps leading into Eduardo's.

He was wise enough not to enter the dim room after being exposed to the direct sunlight so he planted his right leg on the top step, folded his arms across his knee, listened to the painful appeal beyond the door, and waited for the Outlaw to emerge so they could stand face to face on equal terms.

He had seen the likes of many bandits in the towns he had regulated and his patience had long since departed from his skill traits, however within he knew he had never stood in the way of a man with the deadly reputation of 'The Outlaw'.

At first, he hesitated confronting the Outlaw. For a few minutes he had stayed behind his desk in the safety of his office staring at the wanted poster. He had deliberated shooting down the hated man from behind cover because he knew he was no longer as quick with the trigger or as sure with his aim as he once was, but wrestling with his conscience, he also knew he was no coward.

Smoke drifted upwards from his cigar as he spoke without removing the tobacco stub.

"Ok. Now she's done I'm going do some talking," Sheriff Gisty was taking no chances and he had withdrawn and levelled his pistol in the direction of the door, now his aim was fixed on the Outlaw. "And you're going to do some listening."

"I'm all ears sheriff." The Outlaw casually smiled.

"You're going to do exactly as I say."

The likeness of the wanted posters did not depict the menace in the killer's eyes.

"Can't make any promises."

The Outlaw leisurely walked away from the door and stepped out onto the boards. His eyes quickly scanned both directions of the near-deserted, silent street and he smiled at the half-hidden faces of the enthused, the nervous, and the fearing.

"Get your hands up and move back against that wall."

Gisty waved the barrel of his pistol to show in which direction he wanted the Outlaw to move.

"I'm not heading in that direction sheriff." The Outlaw continued his gait towards the Arabian.

"Now you are." Gisty took a few cautious steps forward.

"I'm afraid that badge you're wearing there sheriff don't pay you enough to tell me what to do."

"Money matters to me none." Gisty knew his hope of detainment with a peaceful resolution was unlikely. He spat out the remnants of the cigar near his feet and without breaking from the stare he exterminated the heat with the sole of his boot.

"It don't?" laughed the Outlaw. "Well, all the same, I think a man of your age should choose a safer profession."

"And miss bringing the likes of you to justice." Gisty riposted. "Now that's enough talking, Outlaw."

A bead of sweat ran down his cheeks and glistened. "Get your hands up and get em up high."

"Well now sheriff, you seem to be a likable type of a man and I don't want to kill you, but I'm not turning myself in today." The Outlaw raised his right hand and lowered the brim of his vaquero with a tap from his fingers. "Because you see that nice lady who passed you by just now, well she has just given me a reason to live a while longer."

Gisty glanced at the bag of coins in his left hand and took a step forward.

"Why you son of a bitch! You'd take from the devil himself to buy yourself another day on this earth." He stiffened his outstretched arm and firmed his grip on the pistol. "I'm taking you in so drop the belt and get your hands up."

"You're not listening to me sheriff," the Outlaw ignored the menace of steel and neared the hitch rail. "I can't and I won't be yielding today."

"Can't or won't. It don't make any difference." Gisty began to pull on the trigger. "You're coming with me, either on your feet or on your back."

"Well then let me just help you change your ways of thinking."

Two explosions erupted within an instant, smoke blasted thick and the sheriff dropped his gun and fell to the floor. He screamed and writhed in pain clasping both his hands around his foot.

Blood welled through his leather boot and his fingers.

The Outlaw casually holstered the Tranter, kicked away the sheriff's smoking pistol, then took the reins to calm the agitated Arabian. Once in the saddle, he pulled the horse to the centre of the street.

"Now don't you go make me turn around." He said, looking down at the impaired lawman. "You did your best. Now let it be."

Chapter 4

Gazing up at the dark velvet sky, Liberty May was thinking about running away. Fleeing far away from Rio Rojo was deep-rooted in her thoughts throughout every moment of the brightest day and the longest of nights.

Although she had plenty to run away from, she had nowhere to run to. Foolish to stay, she lacked the courage which she must summon one day for her survival when circumstances and her instincts would dictate that her only chance of hope and salvation was to escape from the cruelty and torment which was being inflicted upon her by her evil stepfather, Macklin Bucks.

Liberty May did not belong on West Valley ranch, two miles south of Rio Rojo, she never belonged there. She hated the ranch, the town and her stepfather, all of whom hated her back in equal terms.

She had never been welcomed or accepted by anyone in the county because of the colour of her skin. From her first arrival in the dusty trading town, hardened prejudices faced her at every turn. Liberty May was only four years old when American troopers unexpectedly galloped, as the sun rose, into the small camp of the Caddo tribe and exterminated every man, woman, and child.

Had the misled soldiers not attacked when most were still asleep on that fateful morning, they would have been welcomed by the peacefull Caddos.

They were an unaggressive family who lived peacefully on the distant cedar hills.

The Caddos lived off the land and traded hand-stitched hides to the merchants, seldom did they have any contact with outsiders or settlers who flooded the region to erect wooden towns and trading posts at pace. However, their peaceful existence suddenly changed when reports of Indian attacks spread fast and panic unnerved the press, the Governor and other various decision makers in the surrounding counties.

Eager for military action and to cut through general boredom, Captain George Stonehouse led out the Texas Rangers to cleanse the region of all regarded hostiles. Without consideration or apathy, seventy-two Caddos were innocently executed as a new spring dawn began. Only two of the Caddo family survived, a white woman and her infant daughter.

A vigilant sergeant and conscientious objector to the slaughter noticed the white-skinned woman dressed in deerskin arched over protecting her small child. The soldier shielded the woman and her child from the hail of bullets, lances and swords and escorted them to safety after the cleansing of the camp was completed.

The sergeant reported to his superior, however the woman refused to answer any of the captain's questions and being infuriated by her apparent lack of gratification from being freed from her captivity he ordered the sergeant to escort the two females to the nearest town where they would be rehabilitated into civilised society.

The soldier's assumption of her capture was incorrect. Years earlier the Denson family were travelling south where Joseph Denson was planning to invest in his brother's printing business in the rapidly expanding mining towns.

However, the hastily arranged venture soon faulted.

As the family travelled over the unforgiving plains Joseph, his wife and eldest child fell ill and soon perished, however as the youngest daughter was taking her final breaths and seemingly not going to reach her eighth year, a wandering Indian hunter saw what he thought was an abandoned schooner.

Inquisitively he peered inside the canvas and saw the three dead bodies and the seriously ill child still cradled in the arms of her dead mother. After cremating the dead, the Indian rounded up the loose oxen and drove the wagon and the dying girl back to Cedar Hills to return to his tribe.

Using tribal remedies the girl's health improved and she was adopted by a childless couple with whom she lived with serenity until she married a Caddo boy.

Almost one year later the white woman with dark red hair and green eyes gave birth to a girl of equal splendour however only three further years had passed when the massacre occurred.

At first the sergeant could not persuade any of the citizens of Rio Rojo to help the teenager and her small child. The mother and daughter were repelled with every enquiring knock.

Money and food were scarce and the locals had learnt to be frugal, no one wanted two extra mouths to feed especially the one with the shaded skin. Nearing despair and annoyance the soldier pleaded with the town's new reverend who eventually, after being persuaded by his Christian and warm-hearted wife, who considered nurturing as their duty and God's will, agreed to give food and shelter to the pair until they could be fostered by a more prosperous suitor.

Four more years were to pass before that suitor arrived on the pastor's doorstep. Macklin 'Mac' Bucks was a local rancher who had a huge homestead at the edge of town. Recently widowed and without family he was struggling to manage his household affairs.

He offered to take in Liberty May, named by the pastor's wife because the young Indian girl was now free from captivity and it was the month of May when they arrived with the soldier, and her mother Ruby May, also named by the pastor's wife because of her dark red hair, to live with him on the ranch and work as housekeepers.

He vowed to give them both a good Christian life in return for their labours and that same evening the pastor defied his wife's objections and helped Macklin Bucks transport Ruby May and her child, Liberty May, the two-mile journey to his ranch at West Valley.

Labour-gruelling days dragged into restless nights for Ruby and Liberty May. Macklin Bucks offered nothing except hard work for the privilege of rude shelter and scant food.

He, along with most of the other men in Rio Rojo, despised Liberty May for the colour of her skin and to ensure Ruby obliged him by performing her duties in the homestead he feigned harmony and affection.

He tolerated being teased by the locals whilst in retaliation he vented his cowardly frustration by working the girl hard on the farmstead with chores more suited to experienced ranchers and too frequently when his mean spirit was fuelled with liquor-tainted prejudices and bitterness he took to beating the girl and her mother with his strap.

Eventually Ruby married Mac, not out of love or duty, she reluctantly and shrewdly tied the deed for security and personal gains. She wanted to secure an inheritance for her now teenage daughter and pleasing Mac with a happy marriage was a risk she was willing to take. Unfortunately, Ruby's ambition was equalled by the wily old rancher and he harboured secret desires of his own.

Once married, he hoped for a blessing from God as his reward for offering habitation to the young savages and he prayed prior to lusting because he wanted the blessing to be in the form of his own child.

However, as often in the cruel west, his hopes were soon crushed and his future plan destroyed. Ruby suddenly fell ill and within weeks, her ailments reduced her to a skeletal shell with a lingering death.

Mac was inconsolable, not that he truly loved Ruby, he considered her as a vessel to carry and raise his family and he treated her as one of his belongings, a necessity, useful and needed, but not loved or respected and he knew that finding another adequate woman in La Vaca County would be impossible.

After the funeral he faced a dilemma, what to do with Liberty May. Abandon the teenager and discard her to the streets to toil for her own survival or cash in by offering her hand in marriage to a suitor who was willing to heavily pay Mac recompense for his investment with fostering, educating and civilising the Indian girl.

The homestead's suffering did not cease with just the departure of Ruby. The onset and consequences of the civil war had ravaged the region in the few years since her death, West Valley's livestock had been appropriated by the rebel army and trade had plummeted with the cost of feed inflating beyond control.

Throughout the region, stock had become scarce as pilfering desperate soldiers took whatever they could carry resulting in evaporating incomes and inadequate prosperity.

Currency became almost worthless overnight and almost everyone who stayed in La Vaca County became broke with a bleak future.

The unforeseen plight fixed Mac's mind despite him knowing that finding suitors who could offer tempting recompense for the security of marriage would prove difficult.

Many single men of marrying age had already left the town to kill Yankees and almost all others lacked appeal or resources and being desperate for funds they offered no bait worth consideration. However, when word spread of Mac's intentions two suitors soon became smitten and enchanted by the appeal of the tanned girl with long shiny auburn locks.

Mainly because of their lack of finesse, their well-known brutal nature and unappealing visage, both men were dull in the presence of females and they lacked any natural allure and sophistication. They failed to attract the eye of the local maidens looking for love and marriage and so Liberty May was a prize worth haggling for.

Mac knew both men would not make suitable husbands and any self-respecting father would distance their daughters from the pair, however he did not care about Liberty May's prospects and his considerations were for wholly selfish gains.

Charles Tillman was the son of a fellow rancher five miles across the plains. Tillman enlisted into the local militia and soon became captain. He controlled affairs in Rio Rojo and he dominated the needy who had suffered because of the war. He protected his father's homestead by using militia men as security against scavenging deserters and he abused his position by securing provisions whilst negotiating unfair, but favourable, trading prices with his compatriots in the army despite the counties' surrounding competitors suffering irreversible damage.

The only other man prepared to bid for the half-breed was an older businessman who had been married before. Known for his enjoyment of liquor and the subsequent evil behaviours which afterwards followed its liberal consumption, Aubrey Willis was a destructive agonistic drunk.

With his fortune secured in the east, young Willis travelled America's frontiers seeking adventure and thrills. He stumbled into Rio Rojo after he overstayed his welcome in Austin and after initially planning only to stay for a few days of recuperation he became attracted to one of the local hurdy girls.

Being flashy by nature and supplied with substantial wealth Willis began to impress the red-haired harlot Charlotte Mace, known as Lottie to her clients, with wild spending to flourish her every requirement beyond anything the townsfolk of Rio Rojo had witnessed before.

Suspicions and judgements of skulduggery were associated with Willis when Lottie's lover and the owner of the brothel was found in an alleyway with a bullet in his back. No witnesses came forth and Sheriff Gisty found no one who could recollect Willis's whereabouts at the time of the incident.

Judge Bechstein ordered Gisty to drop all investigations when an unexpected large donation of cash from Willis was bequeathed to build a new courthouse and less than a month after the man's death Willis had also purchased the whorehouse. He renamed it Red's Casa De Delicia and appointed Lottie as the Madam.

In the following months, Willis began to purchase more properties and businesses along Main Street until he owned the majority of the land and surrounding enterprises.

However, Lottie's and Willis's bliss was short-lived. Often drunk and jealous, Willis persistently argued and harassed Lottie then, as was his routine in the sobering days after an argument, he sought her forgiveness and to regain her favouritism by lavishing her with expensive gifts.

Regularly she displayed the most expensive jewellery that Willis's money could buy alongside the bruises of his wrath. In particular, she vainly flaunted on her cleavage a lavish gold and garnet necklace in which dazzling diamonds blazed her initials 'LM' until one day after another violent and drunken argument Lottie disappeared and was never heard from again.

In the two years since Lottie's disappearance, Willis had become a despised drunk who persecuted his landlords and tenants with inflated rental prices. Most, especially the few ladies of Rio Rojo, avoided contact with the abuser and often crossed the street to thwart having to exchange insincere pleasantries and greetings with the man.

Both Charles Tillman and Aubrey Willis were aware of each other's intentions to wed Liberty May and numerous arguments and threats of injury and death were exchanged on a regular basis between the two rivals.

Jealousy veined through both men in equal measure, but they both lacked the courage needed to end the rivalry man to man. Although Tillman was a vehement bully he relied on the support of his father and the militia to quell any dissidents, while Willis was a coward who slyly lurked in the shadows enacting his maliciousness on the poor with the power of his wealth.

Often igniting the feud from a distance, Mac enjoyed the privileges of being the father of the bride-to-be and often played one off against the other. As both men raged and tried to discredit one another, they shared with Mac inducements from the gains of their prosperity and power to secure favour and seek advantage over one another in a bid to entice Mac into making his preferred choice.

All the time Mac revelled in the benefits the rivals bestowed upon him, he drank and ate for free in Willis's bars and he enjoyed the company of complimentary women in his bordello. His fortunes prospered with donations placed into his bank account by Willis with the promise of more to follow when he would finally be considered family and he was given personal protection by the militia, often walking shoulder to shoulder with them when he visited Rio Rojo.

The militia's protection extended to West Valley's animals and stocks and they were guarded day and night from opportunist plunderers whilst they liberally stole from the vulnerable and deprived.

Mac also used his leverage with Tillman to gain an advantage over his competitors by using the militia to confiscate seed and feed from neighbouring farmers in order to maintain his last remaining livestock and smoothly aid in operating his beloved ranch through the uncertain war years.

The citizens of Rio Rojo who once pitied the unfortunate Mac Bucks now despised him and secretly wished him ill fortune. Although they frowned upon the half-savage girl they despised his blatant exploitation and his ill-gained advantage over the farming community and competition.

While Mac enjoyed the privileges bestowed upon him by the two desperate adversaries he knew he was still only months away from financial ruin.

The fortunate few in the south who still had money, cattle and horses found it impossible to sell their goods for profit, and even when the army did not commandeer the beasts their payment terms were issued as worthless credit notes.

Mac knew if he wanted to keep his lands and run a business he needed to survive well beyond Lee's imminent surrender and so he intended to reap the benefits provided by the suitors for as long as possible.

Until that day arrived he decided to instigate and inflict one more act of final cruelty upon Liberty May.

"No customers again tonight," said Daisy Dufran, the new madam of the Casa De Delicia.

She cast a scowl to confirm she knew Liberty May was doing all she could to avoid company rather than trying to entice and attract punters with the lurid teases which the other whores in the Casa De Delicia had perfected.

"Mac won't be happy again."

"I don't care. I'm not laying with no sweaty-backed man." Liberty May stood erect with her arms folded signalling her defiance. "No matter how much silver they swank in with and no matter how many times that asshole whips me." Her stern barrier could not prevent the display of her emotional pain.

Daisy had seen this resistance many times before then again she knew desperation always conquered and subdued the embarrassment and pain.

Normally she offered no sympathy or help, she cared little for the brothel girls who were there to satisfy the carnal needs of the opportune licentious.

They had all recounted tales of misfortune which led them through the door into this profession, however with Liberty May apathy did tug upon her conscience resulting in slightly favourable allowances.

"I'm afraid it's only a matter of time, my dear." She sighed.

"I'm not going to do it. I do not belong in a place like this."

"Yeah, yeah." Daisy breathed as she wiped slops from the highly polished bar.

She did not argue, she knew the constant bullying would eventually prevail and the poor girl would succumb to the pressure just as the other wives and widows, who now draped themselves half-naked over the large leather chairs and silk chaises, had.

Money was always the winner in this town, and now it was a privilege for only a few.

Despite the sympathy, Daisy did nothing to urge Liberty May to relent. Deep down she did not want the half-Indian girl in her parlour, it wasn't that Liberty was unattractive, her splendour easily attracted the eye of the non-prejudiced enquirer.

Mac stopped at the complementary bar ignoring Daisy's attempt to take the conversation into her private room at the rear of the building.

"It's not Libby's fault." She excused.

"Not her fault eh?" Mac breathed alcohol into her face.

"We haven't had anyone come through the doors again." She remonstrated holding firm her stance as he swayed in front of her.

"And when they do." He forced his red-veined eyes to within inches of her face. "Do you think they'll come looking for a squaw cooze!" He raised his finger over his rear and pointed at the sultry-dressed yet natural-faced girl. "Look at her! Who in these parts is willing to pay for a savage?"

For a moment the silence was only broken by the popping flames of the lanterns and candles, and scowls flashed amongst the resentful who thought their earnings were jeopardised by the mongrel.
Liberty May lowered her face as all the eyes in the room slanted towards her direction.

"Get some flour paint and cover that god-darn red skin!" he raged, grabbing a whisky bottle from the meagre stock of beverages and then staggered over to where Liberty May was leaning.
"Nobody wants to even look at a squaw, never mind pay scarce dough to roll with one."

As the insult left his mouth, a loud slap from the flat of his hand followed. Liberty May's neck stretched and her body pivoted around, leaving her to clumsily stumble backwards and collide with a credenza and then fall into the gaudy draperies. Ornaments rattled and candlesticks swayed as she shielded her face.

"Clumsy bitch!" cursed one of the unsympathetic whores, springing forwards to prevent a large candelabrum from falling.

Seeing Mac clench his fist through her fingers, Liberty May reeled sidewards expecting another blow to land on the forming white hand imprint on her cheek.

"Stop!" Daisy screeched, grabbing with both her hands Mac's retracting arm. "Don't you dare damage the goods!" She shouted, putting her body between the stunned girl and the drunk.

"Bitch needs a good whipping." he slurred, his eyes widening from the distraction of Daisy's lively bosom.
"Nobody's going to buy a bruised peach when there are other fruits in the basket to choose from."

Daisy stood defiant, opening her hand in the direction of the gawking whores. Inwardly she was enraged, not just by Mac's bullying and overbearing manner, but by her own and Liberty May's passive acceptance of this humiliation. Her mouth contracted tight and her pallid skin blanched paler.

"Arr go git, you're not worth the effort." Mac raised the bottle to his lips and turned away from Liberty May to face the bemused onlookers.

All their eyes diverted from his gaze in an effort to avoid his interest.

Unfortunately, Daisy's bosom had aroused Mac's appetite; he scanned across the room until he fixed upon another girl whose tight-fitting bodice also enhanced her half-exposed breasts.

"You, what's your name?" He pointed towards the blonde wig wearer. She did not answer.
"Come here." He arched out his arm to welcome her.

She failed to comply and Daisy tilted her head and widened her eyes at Mac's chosen companion. "Come on Beulah. You full well know how to behave for our patrons."

Her signal was received with a sigh and, reluctantly, Beulah slowly arose from the chaise. Mac's eyes dropped down to her swaying buttocks as she turned to grab a lounging robe, and he released a saliva-dripping smile as she swayed.

"Lordy oh Lordy." he grinned, folding his arm tightly around her slender waist as she neared him. "Let us go get some fun." he leered, pressing his drooling lips against her warm cheek.
"Bring me another bottle up." he demanded of Daisy as he leant on the much smaller woman to angle her towards the stairwell.

"And get that bitch painted!" he scowled hatred over his shoulder. "Then figure a way of getting some men in here."

He wobbled and hesitated at the stairwell. "If you don't plant some greenbacks in my palm pretty soon I'll be doing some talking with Mr Willis."

Holding him steady and guiding his feet onto the polished wooden steps, Beulah was experienced enough to know the only pleasure Mac was going to receive tonight would be in the form of a comfy mattress as he slept off a drunken stupor. She winked and smiled at Liberty May as she hauled him up the stairs.

Chapter 5

Low clouds blocked the silver moon glow and the night shadows allowed the Outlaw to edge up within twenty feet of the Confederate sentry.

The half-conscious guard rested with his back against the trunk of a thick elm and his musket at ease against his folded arms. Through exhausted slits, he numbly stared into the darkness, failing in his duty to keep an ardent watch.

For the last three weeks, the Outlaw had tracked the regiment of the 4th Texas Infantry north, then east. He followed the soldiers' tracks of destruction through ravaged farms, pilfered homesteads and trails of rotting corpses.

At the edge of a gunpowder-reeking and smog-hanging large forest, Mattie Darrell's bag of coins had loosened the tongues of the stubborn and suspicious locals, making it easy for the Outlaw to close in on the fighting unit of men while they rested.

Here, foul-tasting air soured the northern breeze, and the Outlaw had to stoop low in the foliage and gulp repeatedly for pine scent to clear his lungs of carbon and ease his powder-smarting eyes.

He turned an eye to far distant thunder, he counted between the blasts until he realised the rupture in the northern sky and the lightning flares was not approaching, nor was it thunder.

The rumble some miles away was a distant cannonade being unleashed to wield its powerful destruction and prevent sleep and rest on the battle-weary enemy.

Brambles cracked beneath his feet as he stepped out from the cover of the foliage.

"Whoa!" The sound jolted the bleary-eyed camp sentry. "Who goes there?" He levelled his rifle toward the approaching shadow.

"Lower your shooter, friend," the Outlaw called out.

"I will not." he sure'd his aim.

"Well then, hold your finger steady on that trigger."

"What you doing sneaking around out there in the dark?" The soldier blinked repeatedly to focus his vision. "You a Yank?"

"Far from it, fella. I was born to the soil of Texas."

"Well I'll ask ya again. What you slinking about out there in the dark?" The soldier curled and firmed his fingers around the trigger.

"I'm looking for my brother." the Outlaw lied, slowly stepping nearer to reveal himself.

"Get your hands up where I can see em." He stretched out the rifle a few inches to try to discourage the stranger from approaching. "Come on now get em up high and don't move."

"I've got news from back home."

"Yeah."

"Yeah." The Outlaw began to slide his hand inside his jacket.

"I said don't move." The soldier moved his right foot forward to firm his stance. "I'll shoot," he warned. "I ain't afraid to drop you." He held the rifle firm until the trigger clicked. "The Capt says I'm to shoot first and ask questions later. He doesn't take lightly to Yanks or runners." His voice hinted at a lack of astuteness.

"Well, as I've already told you, I'm no Yank, and I sure as hell ain't no coward." The Outlaw continued to slowly reach inside his jacket. "I've got a letter for my little brother."

"I'm warning you! Don't come any closer or you'll be shitting out lead," the soldier demanded, and he squinted at the stranger's hand as it pulled free from inside his coat, a piece of paper.

"I'm looking for Bobby Ray Darell of the 4th Texas. I just come to give him news from back home." He held the note up above his head. It fluttered in the breeze.

"Well, you can't come into camp. Orders is orders, so just turn right on back around and go get back to where you come from."

"I can't do that." The Outlaw shook his head.

"I've warned you once, mister, and I ain't about to do it again."

"Look, friend, I just need to get this note to my brother."

Another forward step was taken. "I ain't asking for much… you see it's bad news, real bad."

A break in the clouds allowed the moonlight to reveal the soldier's face. The Outlaw noted his youthful vulnerability and smiled.

"Well then, you just leave it on that there stone over yonder, and I'll take it into camp come sunup." He motioned with the rifle and pointed the barrel at a large flat boulder.

"I can't do that." Again, the Outlaw shook his head, and he took another deliberate step forward. "You see, these are the last words of our dear mama, written in her own hand for her youngest as she lay on her deathbed." Another step was taken as he continued. "She made me promise to find him and deliver it personally before he could be taken by a Yankee bullet."

The Outlaw noticed the soldier's brow furrow as he speculated.

"I've come too far to fail her now." He held the note high above his head.

"What you say his name is?" he shouted above the distant rumble of cannon fire.

"Bobby Ray Darell. Everyone back home just calls him young Bob."

Still the Outlaw inched forward.

"You see, when he left home he was only this high." The Outlaw's arm aligned with his chest.

"I don't recall I heard that name before, and besides, he's probably resting alongside his mama now, because the 4th took a hell of a whooping out there today and ain't but half of them returned to camp."

The lookout's rifle began to tilt downwards as he compassionately shook his head.

"Darn it. I figured I might be too late. I scooted up here as fast as my legs would carry me."

The Outlaw now stood directly in front of the young soldier. He lamented a sigh to feign regret. "We all told him his courage wouldn't keep him alive when the lead started hailing."

"I'm sorry n'all," the soldier shook his head.

"You still got your mama, son?"

The Outlaw toyed with the young man's conscience. He knew most southern boys' hearts carried a particular fondness for their creator, especially when they were far away from home and facing death with the prospect of treading God's staircase with every sunrise.

"Guess you're making her real proud… just like our young Bob did."

A passing cloud allowed the moon to briefly reveal the willingness which eased on the soldier's face.

"I guess I can ask the fellas back in camp come the morn." The soldier offered. "What you say his name was again?"

The Outlaw held out the note in front of the soldier, who unwittingly took the bait and released his left arm from the barrel and stretched out his hand to meet the paper.

The rifle now hung limp, pointing downwards, and as another blast of cannon fire caused the soldier to shudder, the Outlaw swiftly withdrew his pistol and smashed its steel against the youngster's head.

The crack of steel against bone was muffled by the young man's kepi, and only the rustle of foliage sounded as the unconscious soldier dropped limp to the floor.

The Outlaw glanced in all directions to check if the conversation had roused any interest. Other than the distant cannon claps, undisturbed stillness lay in the immediate area of the lookout post.

He stripped the young boy of his jacket, kepi, and rifle and, for a moment, considered slicing open the boy's throat. But knowing the blow would render him senseless until after sunup, he opted not to end his life and give him the chance of succumbing to an honourable death at the hands of the blue bellies. Donning the drab fighting colours of the South, the Outlaw stepped forth into the eerie atmosphere where the presence of death and suffering hung deep around the hue of the surrounding campfires.

Hardship, desolation, blood, and pain were etched deep into the silent faces that squatted around the flames, looking for solace and reflection from the warmth of the dancing firelight.

A distant flute and fiddle could be heard. Inaptly, it failed to raise the spirits of the desolated mourners and the souls of those whose morning prospects looked dim.

Many sat silent, smoking their homemade pipes, reminiscing of kinder days not too long ago, whilst others angled letters and books towards the flames to distract themselves in vain with words of comfort from faraway places where the grim reaper was not welcomed.

The Outlaw ignored the glassy-eyed daydreamers, wounded and inconsolable, as he walked unnoticed in the solemn presence of death. He held the tin plate of the boy against the light of the flames and occasional malodorous kerosene lamps which swayed from chains, and he repeatedly called out the name.

"Bob Darell… Bob Ray Darell… Bobby Ray Darell… has anybody seen this boy?"

Still, he received only unresponsive gazes, inaudible grunts, and the occasional shaking of heads. He crouched down beside a solitary tobacco-chewing old timer and held the tin plate up to his face.

"I've got a message for Bobby Ray Darell of the Texas 4th."

The old man did not respond. His eyes were fixed on the mesmerising ambers, his jaw moving only to gnaw on a tobacco leaf.

"Have you seen him?" The Outlaw hovered the picture between the old man and the firelight.

"Bob who?" came a call from an unseen face at the other side of the blaze.

"Bobby Ray Darell. A youngster from La Vaca County." The Outlaw raised himself. "I've got a message for him." He peered over the fire at the other man. "Have you seen him?"

"Not that I recall. The last I heard was that the survivors of the 4th were squatting at the far end of the camp, way over on yonder."

A raised hand and a straightened finger pointed to the Outlaw's right. "Just keep on walking about five hundred clicks."

"Thank ya kindly," he replied, scanning across the stretch of darkness which was pierced only by intermittent swinging lanterns.

"That's if there are any of the poor suckers left," the voice from beyond the flames bewailed.

The Outlaw helped himself to a ladle of root stew and then turned away from the smoke. He carefully placed his feet around the weary, wounded, dead, and dying until he could step furtively, unobserved, around the edge of the camp in the shadows of hastily arranged tents.

"Bob Darell… Bob Ray Darell… Bobby Ray Darell," he repeated the calls when he estimated he was close to the area of the 4th. However, he met the same blank responses from the array of similarly expressionless faces until, after a few more minutes of appealing, someone hailed out of the darkness.

"Who wants to know?"

"Andrew Darell, his brother," the Outlaw misled.

"Bobby Ray from down in La Vaca County?" the faceless voice queried.

"The same… born and raised in Rio Rojo."

"Brother, you say?" drawled the soldier.

"I did."

"And your business?" he asked.

"I've got a letter from his mama." The Outlaw held aloft the paper in the dimness, knowing no one could see clearly. "She begged me to deliver her final words just before she passed."

He repeated the tale of woe again to appeal to the soldier's sensitive emotions.

"Dog tent at the far end of the row over there." A cloud of grey tobacco smoke bellowed from the darkness. "Least he was in there last time I saw him," he shouted at the pause of nearby cannon thunder.

"Much obliged to you, soldier." The Outlaw gestured his thanks by waving the paper.

Then, tucking it back inside his jacket, he turned to walk towards the row of tents.

"Pretty shot up, so I'm not sure he will still be with us," the sightless soldier added as the Outlaw disappeared.

Again, he navigated through the semi-darkness until he reached a line of dead bodies.

He paused momentarily, knowing he would not be able to compare the tin plate in the intermittent moonlight against the swollen death grimaces, so he moved on towards the small scattering of tents. Exhibiting lanterns to the front, he hoped these small islands of light denoted life.

He arched low to peer through a small tear in the tattered canvas. In the dimness he could just see four prostrate bodies and nothing else.

Putrid air seared his nostrils, and he turned his head back to the night air to refresh his lungs and draw breath before he ventured inside.

He reached up to unhook an oil lantern from the post, then pulled open the canvas and angled his shoulder to slip inside the tent.

The sweetness of blood fouled his nostrils, and he reacted by holding the back of his free hand up to shield his nose from the death reek. He held the lamp above the four bodies.

There was no squinting from the sudden light or moans from the disturbance, there was no reaction of any type from the blood-drenched men.

Clasping onto their last salvation, bibles lay on their chests, and laudanum bottles were fixed in their grips as they forfeited their lives and prayed to release their final pained breath.

One of the bodies gurgled, and the Outlaw turned to face the corner of the tent. He lowered the linen face covering, which was damp with darkened saliva.

"Bobby Ray?" whispered the Outlaw, bending over the man for a closer inspection. "Is that you, Bob?"

The light from the lantern jolted the man, and he squirmed, muttering deliriously without opening his eyes. A stream of blood appeared from the side of his mouth. Only words were prevented because his lower jaw had been shattered, and it was held firm with a crude binding.

"Is that you, pap's?" The call prompted the Outlaw to turn around again to see a ruffling beneath a pile of discarded rebel jackets.

"Bobby Ray?" The Outlaw's brow furrowed.

"Pap's?" An ashen face appeared from beneath the rags.

"I'm not your papa, Bob. I'm a friend who's gonna get you out of here."

The Outlaw crouched beside the partially covered boy.

He slid his hand across the boy's forehead to remove grimy blood; the coldness of the boy's skin caused him to retract it fast.

"They shot me, Pa." The boy's voice was feeble and his breathing shallow.

The Outlaw nodded. "You've got a bad fever there, Bob."

He knew he did not have to check the tin plate for a likeness; he had found Bob Ray Darell. Although fragile and deranged, he was still alive.

"Got me real bad," the boy moaned.

"Hush now. Save your strength, Bob." The Outlaw calmed Bob by placing his palms on his shoulders. "I'm going to take you home."

"For some of Mama's apple pudding." A delicate smile creased through the grimace of pain.

"That's right, Bob. A good helping of your mama's special."

"Oh, I can smell it from here, Pap's." The smile gave way to a cringe of pain.

"Hush now and lay still until I get back."

He covered Bob with a layer of jackets and returned to the camp. Whilst the troop found solace by gazing into fires, drowsing in reminiscent slumbers, inspecting their weapons, reading words from home and newspaper snippets, the Outlaw walked among them in search of a stretcher.

However, after tipping out a collection of logs, he returned to the makeshift tent to haul the lightweight and now unconscious frame of the boy into a crude wheelbarrow.

"What you got going on there, soldier?" asked an observant and suspicious corporal.

"I found the boy a nice resting place under an oak just over by the stream back there." The Outlaw carefully put the cart to rest and pointed into the black wilderness.

"You gonna end up digging a lot of holes if that's your way of figuring, soldier."

The colonel had seen too many dead, and he gave only a cursory glance to the ashen-faced figure.

"No, sir. This stream ain't that pretty, sir." He shook his head, dismissing the colonel's notion. "I knew this little fella from when he was still in shorts. Just reckon I owe it to his family to set him somewhere nice and peaceful."

"Well, I admire your sentiment, soldier, but you need to hurry on and get some rest in." The colonel began to walk away. "We've got a big day come sunup."

"Yes, sir. I'll be back in no time at all."

The Outlaw lied as he lifted and moved forward with the cart with ease. Then, avoiding all restlessness and activity, he left the smoke and flames of the campfires behind him to disappear into the mass of black timbers.

"Funny thing that," Bob prised open an eyelid.

"What?" The Outlaw questioned with shock at the unexpected words.

"They don't take no time to tune up and start singing again once the cannons stop." Bob was shaking against the side of the carriage as the timber wheel bounced hard over protruding and obstructing roots.

The Outlaw paused and glanced around him, then angled his face towards the darkened treetops. A smile narrowed his eyes, and he shook his head as his ears filled with the tunes of birdsong instead of cannonade. Darn it, the boy's right, he mused.

Chapter 6

Silence descended rapidly around the boardwalks and the street corners of Rio Rojo as the man with the long shadow led his horse from the distant scorched hills into the town and by the church.

With the dazzling afternoon sun to his rear, squinting eyes and shielding hands could not help the onlookers identify the man leading his horse by the reins. Adding to the growing and speculating interest, a smaller man was slouched across the saddle.

Fading dust left a trace of their path leading from the faraway hills and down the slope to the church. It rose easily in their wake from the hard sunbaked soil.

Doors began to inch, shutters creaked, and the presence of the curious increased as speculation aroused amongst the loitering citizens who had no means of occupation and little to do on the scorching afternoons except reminisce of more prosperous times and waste the daylight hours with idle gossip.

"Oh my God," a woman drawled through her hand just loud enough so that only those around her could hear her astonishment.

"Is that…" began another woman as the man on foot, the white horse, and the unconscious rider drew level. "Young Bob Darell?"

With the face-concealing shadows now cleared, the onlookers had a sure view of the young Confederate who was strapped over the impressive Arabian's mane. Dripping blood spoiled the striking pure coat and caused concern amongst the multiplying numbers of gazers.

"Isn't that the… the Outlaw?" was whispered.

The Outlaw was familiar with the whispered, curious, and fearing welcomes which he received whenever he chose to show himself, and he walked unabated with his back straight and his gaze forward.

"He's brought him back!" someone shrieked.

He ignored the mutterings and continued on with the reins in his hand, looking straight ahead and only occasionally slanting his grey eyes in the direction of the static inquisitive who gathered in the shadows of the terracing.

"Is he alive?"

The muted observations continued.

"I don't believe what I am seeing."

The townsfolk didn't know whether to celebrate Bob's return or run in fear of their lives.

"We've got to go get Mattie."

The Outlaw tethered the Arabian to the hitch rail outside Eduardo's Barra de Tequila, just as he had four weeks earlier.

He flashed a glance in both directions of the street and across the dirt to the surrounding buildings.

He smirked as he saw someone flip the closed sign on the bank door and, after locking it, pull down the blind.

From a distance, the tentative and staring still occupied the frontages, windows, and doorways. No one dared to help the wanted man unstrap the binding from around the boy's hands, which were secured to the pommel.

Again the Outlaw cast a carefree scowl at the onlookers before releasing the strapping to slide Bob down from the saddle and onto the dust. Then he hauled the boy over his shoulder and kicked his way through the creaking double doors of the cantina.

The Outlaw paused in the doorway momentarily, allowing his eyes to adjust in the hazy gloom. Again he found the bar empty—almost empty.

One silver-bearded old timer had not fled along with the rest of the crowd, and he remained seated at the gambling table, eyes slanting downwards as he shuffled a deck of cards.

"Kinda lonely playing solitaire. Don't ya think?" said the Outlaw with some amusement.

"You'd be the judge of that," came the quick reply.

"Why you still here?" the Outlaw wondered at the old man's motives for still being seated.

"You got no quarrel with me," he supported his comment by half-raising his palm. "Just too old to run."

"That so." The Outlaw headed towards the nearest high-backed chair.

"Guess it be," the old timer gulped down a shot of whiskey. "Old and stupid."

"Not much you can do about being old," said the Outlaw as he slumped the boy down into the chair and stretched the stiffness from his back. "I figure maybe it's better than the alternative for some." He then angled his head towards the gambling table. "And if you leave your hands above the table, being stupid won't be getting you shot today."

"As I said, you ain't got no quarrel with me." He obliged, raising his hands to show he was holding only cards.

The Outlaw ruffled the unconscious boy's hair and patted him on the shoulder in a friendly way.

For the first time in months, he felt strangely exulted. Completing a good deed was new to him, and the unfamiliar affinity had briefly calmed his inner storm.

He walked around to the business side of the bar and glanced at the few offerings. He saw the Viva Tequila he drank on his last visit, and his face twisted with disapproval. He allowed his hand to drift across the top of the bottles until it rested upon the last one in line.

Tossing his hat onto the bar, he slammed out the cork, then held his head back and filled his mouth so much that he had to gulp three times to swallow the liquor.

"Darn," he rasped, shaking his head as the venom burned his dry throat.

On the bar was a tepid bowl of stew and a half-eaten bread roll. He dipped the roll into the gravy and scooped the food into his mouth, not stopping until the bowl was empty.

"Good?" the old timer asked, observing his eagerness to satisfy his hunger. "Eddie's lady is renowned for her edibles."
"Just about beats berries and roots," he replied, wiping his mouth as he twisted to angle the whisky bottle towards Bob's sun-blistered lips.

The potency of the drop stirred the boy, and his face flinched as, moaning, he shook his head. The Outlaw poured another small dose, and the boy coughed and spluttered, but this time he briefly opened his eyes.

Outside, darkened figures crowded the gangway and jostled to peer through the glass at the activity within the bar.

"Bobby Ray! Bobby Ray!" screamed out from the doorway. "Is that really you?"

Heels pounded against the planks, and Mattie Darell threw herself down on her knees in front of her son. "Is that really you?" She ran her fingers quickly through his hair. "I never thought I'd see you again."

She jerked her head upwards and clasped her hands together to quickly worship the Lord, then she lunged forwards to wrap her arms around the weakling.

"Oh my, oh my. Thank the Lord." Haggard anguish lines seemed to fade from her countenance, and rosiness ruddled her cheeks.

"Ain't the Lord you should be thanking," quipped the old timer, flipping cards.

"You brought him back." She feared her eyes were deceiving her, and looking up at the Outlaw, she hugged the boy hard and cradled him in her wrapping arms.

"Well, if a man gets a solid enough reason to go somewhere or do something, then he might as well go and get on with it." He did not remove his gaze from the bottle.

Neither her plea nor her money appealed to him; it was the venture and the opportunity to defy lawmakers again which had roused his spirits and, for the time being, cast away his appetite for his self-destructive hunger.

"Can you hear me, Bobby?" she softly asked.
"Mama," he groaned, parting open his eyelids.
"Yes Bobby, it's your mama. I've come to take you home." Tears flowed down her cheeks and dripped onto his bloodstained butternut jacket.

"Where am I, mama?" he muttered.

"Your home, son." She wiped his matted hair from his cold, damp brow.

"I'm in pain, mama," he groaned almost silently. "My guts hurt real bad."

"Don't you go worrying about that now." She tentatively opened his jacket and raised the burgundy-soiled shirt. Her expression revealed alarm at the grimness of the wound.

"We'll take care of that, Bobby." She hoped.
"Don't think I'm gonna make it, mama." His eyes rolled white.

"Shush now, sure you are. The Lord didn't bring you all this way across country to let you go and die on us now." She stroked away one of her tears from the side of his face.

"The Lord didn't bring him," hollered out from the direction of the gambling table. "And he sure as hell don't give a hoot."

"Oh my. I can't believe it's true. When they said you'd brought him back, I was sure you'd be carrying an empty soul." Mattie raised a beholden look towards the Outlaw with a sparkle of hope in her watery eyes.

At first, the Outlaw ignored her beam and leant back against the bar with his sole angled on the foot rail.

"Guess we all deserve a little of the Lord's grace from time to time."

Then, after a pause, he referred to the need of tending and healing Bob's wounds. "I'm figuring now his burden is over to you."

"Bless you. I can never thank you enough."

Mattie unexpectedly sprang, and wrapping her arms around him, she sobbed into his neck.

As her nostrils filled with the smell of travel dust, gasps of excitement and astonishment sounded from outside. No one alive had ever stood within a few feet of the killer; now, with widening eyes, all breathing was held as they feared for Mattie's life.

"Whoa!" The Outlaw braced himself, and his body went rigid. Carefully and slowly, he rested his palms on Mattie's slender shoulders to guide her backwards and establish distance between them. "I just want to swill the dust from my gullet with a few drops of whiskey." He ignored her gratefulness.

"Mattie!" yelled out another woman from the doorway. "Is it true?" The woman added, rushing into the barroom.

Seeing her sister stood close to the Outlaw, her rushed momentum faltered; terror seized her, and a sudden dread devoured her brief excitement.

"Yes it is." Mattie beamed her delight. "He's alive, Katie!" She turned back to her boy. "He's alive. Isn't it wonderful?"

Confused by what she had seen, then realising her sister's life was not in immediate peril from the Outlaw, Katie gingerly stepped fully into the barroom, releasing the door to swing and close with its own momentum.

"Mr…." Mattie paused and raised her eyebrows, hoping the Outlaw would declare his name, but when his expression remained firm and his lips unresponsive she continued. "Brought him back to us." She beckoned her sister nearer. "Katie, come please. Help me get Bobby home."

Drawing a deep breath and keeping her eyes on the notorious killer, Katie hesitantly completed the few strides to kneel beside her sister.

"I've brought the cart," Katie rushed, with a tremor that indicated her urgency to get out of the room, and flicking anxious glances at the bad man, she tended to the boy with her sister.

Offering no further help and now unconcerned by the activity at his side, the Outlaw swivelled to turn his back on the women. He swigged from the whiskey bottle, his eyes set on the mirror, watching the sisters clumsily struggle to raise the boy up to his disobedient legs.

"God darn it," the old-timer tossed down his cards. "Can't a man find no sanctuary to relax in this town?"

Bob's screams compelled the card player to finish his drink and screech back his chair before helping the two women haul the boy from the toppling seat, but the sight of a commanding figure in grey uniform filling the doorway stopped them cold, leaving Bob's discarded chair to crash backwards onto the floor.

Silence set as heavy, precise footsteps caused the Outlaw to adjust his angle. The flash of light and glint of silver in front of the confederate indicated to the Outlaw the soldier was holding level his pistol.

"Hands up or die!"

The sisters and the gambler held their positions, and losing all control of their nerves, their jaws gaped, mouths dried, and eyes widened. Only the delirious boy's moaning broke the silence.

The Outlaw seemed unconcerned; he remained unmoved with his eyes studying the tall, thin-faced aggressor in the reflection.

"You heard me, Outlaw," the soldier took one more step to firm his stance. "Get your hands up!" He then repeated the command.

The low sun penetrating the glass to his rear concealed the surety in the Outlaw's eyes. "I ain't gonna raise my hands to no coward who comes at me from the back."

"Well, the way I see it is that you got a choice to make," the intruder said without indecision.

"Put 'em high or take a bullet 'cause either way I'm taking you in, and it won't make any difference to me whether you're breathing or not."

"I ain't gonna be obliging you on either account, soldier." The Outlaw's and soldier's eyes locked in the gleaming reflection from beyond the bar. "I ain't going to be accompanying you anyplace, and I don't feel like dying today."

"Make your choice, killer, 'cause your luck has finally run out. Your days breaking the laws of the Almighty are over." The soldier spat a globule towards the feet of the gambler.

"I believe the choice is yours," replied the Outlaw, his voice calm and clear. "Either start shooting or turn around and walk away whilst you can."

"Cut him loose, Tillman," the old gambler voiced up. "Can't you see he's just brought the boy home?"

"Oh, I see alright. Assisting a yella runaway," Tillman scorned, a quick glance towards the blood-drenched youngster. "Another charge to add to the list."

"My boy is a whole lot braver than you," Mattie defended. "Hiding away from the battlefields behind your uniform and rank."

"Shut your hole, woman, or I'll take you down too for harbouring the deserter," Tillman threatened, all the time keeping his gaze on the whiskey drinker who continued to disobey the Captain of the militia.

"Bold and brave, eh?" Still the Outlaw spoke to the reflection. "I've met many of your kind before."

"My kind?"

"The kind who sneaks up from behind with a gun in their hand. The kind that bullies and intimidates young boys and women. The kind that can't fight square."

"Enough!" Tillman raged. "I've heard enough of your barking. Now turn and face me and we'll see who'll fight square."

"Then you'd be making the same mistake that old sheriff made back over in Dry Springs," warned the Outlaw with revealing eyes.

"I don't make mistakes." Tillman held his aim firm and tensed his finger on the trigger.

"Mama... what's... what's happening, mama?" Bob prised open his swollen eyes and rambled.

"Nothing, son." Mattie wiped his brow. "Just rest up now till we get you home."

"Where's the soldier who saved me?" He tried to look at the figures surrounding him; his vision was blurred.

"He's right here beside us." She quickly raised a glance in the direction of the Outlaw, fearing his violent ways were almost over.

She knew Tillman was not brave, yet she knew he was desperate to impress the gullible townsfolk of Rio Rojo, especially one maiden who had caught his eye and whose stepfather he needed to impress.

"He saved my life, mama."

"Yes, he did. Now shush and rest easy." She gently placed her fingers on his lips. "Save your strength, Bobby."

"But I never got to thank him, mama." He rasped through a dry throat.

"No need," she whispered. "He knows."

"Stop your rattling, you little snake." Tillman stamped his foot hard on the boards and switched the angle of his gun. "Before I take to ending your miserable suffering."

Mattie leant her body between Bob and the threat of the pistol.

"All big and mighty, aren't you?" the Outlaw tormented. "Waving your gun around at a boy and a woman."

"Big enough to bring you down, the killer with no name."

"Then I see God blessed you with courage and stupidity in equal measures."

Tillman wasn't courageous; he disguised it with bravado. He normally did his work with the backing of the militia at his side.

Today he had been across the street in the barber's when the fracas interrupted his conversation, and peering through the window he saw the opportunity to capture or kill the wanted man whose back was turned to the door.

Thoughts of revelling in gratitude and esteem occupied his mind and directed his thoughts as he whipped out his pistol, checked its ammunition, and barged through the crowd to enter Eduardo's.

Tillman noticed the slight shift of balance from the Outlaw's feet, and he saw an ominous smile stretch across his mouth in the mirror's reflection. Throat-drying fear panicked him and he pulled hard on the trigger, firing without resetting his aim.

Light flashed, smoke bellowed, and a bullet sped over the Outlaw's shoulder, creating a perfect hole in the glass at the rear of the bar.

"Seems you're having a little trouble shooting straight," said the Outlaw as he spun.

Through the thick smoke Tillman saw death flicker in the Outlaw's grey eyes. Terrified, he pulled hard again on the trigger, and this time both men's pistols erupted flame and thunder simultaneously.

Tillman's gun hand snapped back and his body folded against the wall. With his head still upright, he watched a shower of wicked glass shards fly in all directions as again his shot sped wide of its target.

His eyes gaped wide with shock and pain, and he released a high-pitched scream which lanced everyone's blast-droning ears. Blood spurted high from his shattered right hand, leaving a macabre mural of red on the wall, and through water-filled eyes he watched his loose pistol spin on the planks in front of his knees.

"Go on, make a move for it." Although he no longer savoured death, the Outlaw still teased. "This time I'll split your vitals."

Involuntary shivers ravaged Tillman. Clenching his bloodied fist into a ball, he clasped it with his left hand as he momentarily considered his limited options: reach for the gun and die, or crawl out humiliated in full view of the whole town.

"Make your move and be sure about it," the Outlaw calmly pressed.

Tillman filled his lungs and slid his arm across his eyes to dry the water and clear his vision.

"Now it seems like you've got a choice to make." The Outlaw held firm his aim. Anger simmered beneath his calmness. "Reach for it or go and get it." He narrowed his eyes. "Go and get it or be fed to the buzzards."

Tillman scowled at the motionless women and the gambler, spat to the floor, then staggered to his feet using his shoulder and the wall to steady his balance. He winced and cussed, then without looking at the Outlaw he slowly stumbled towards the door, leaving a trail of blood from the dripping hand.

"I'm as sure as hell you aimed for that hand," the old timer observed.

The Outlaw didn't reply; he simply replaced the used bullet and swivelled back towards the bar.

"Why didn't you kill him?" he petitioned. "And do us all a favour."

"My killing days are done." He holstered the smoking Tranter. "I'm leaving it to the Lord to decide who lives and who dies."

"Well, you better hope your Lord makes his mind up pretty darn quick 'cause Tillman's hurting and he'll come a-hunting you down with a mighty force behind him," the old timer warned. "And now that you've let the whole county know you're here, bounty hunters are going to come flocking from far and wide."

The Outlaw raised the bottle to his lips; the venom still took his breath and he gasped out fumes. "When the Lord and not the Devil comes a-calling, I'll be ready to make my peace."

He wasn't boasting in front of the ladies; his mind was set. He knew he was almost at his fated moment and was prepared to take the step over into the next life to leave all the death and destruction behind him, but today was not that day.

He had decided, at the point where it was almost too late, that he did not want to be killed by Tillman. Tillman was not a warrior who deserved the honour, gratitude, and notoriety for bringing down the most wanted man in Texas.

"Maybe he'll just give me a few minutes of peace to swill out the dust from my throat."

"I wouldn't count on it… a bullet in the back is a bullet in the back whether it's delivered by the Lord or the Devil."

"Darn it." His reply was not a reaction to the old man's words; the bottle was drained. He tossed it down into the covering of glistening shards behind the bar. He decided not to reach for another; it tasted bad—so bad that he couldn't tell the difference between the whiskey and the tequila he drank on his previous visit.

He turned, replaced his hat, and firmed it into position. "Good day." Then he tipped the brim in the direction of the stunned women. "Good day, ladies… Bob."

"Wait!" shouted Mattie.

He ignored her call and walked towards the door without looking back, his steps spreading footprints in the line of fresh blood.

"How can I repay you?"

He lowered his brim further to prevent the brilliance from dazzling his vision. The crowd at the door and window retreated with haste to positions of safety at a distance or behind windows and doors.

He looked down at the trail of blood which led the way to the hitch rail, where it pooled beneath Tillman's dangling arm.

The Outlaw watched the militiaman frantically struggling one-handed to release his rifle from its scabbard. Sweat glistened on his pallid forehead and dampened his shirt.

Without looking, he felt the presence of the Outlaw behind him on the deserted boardwalk, and with one almighty and panicky effort he managed to pull and slide the rifle free from its case. He turned and staggered back against his horse for support, and his momentum enabled him to raise the rifle level with one hand.

The Outlaw now stood before him with an emotionless glare. He calmly rested his hand on the barrel and, applying only minimal pressure, he lowered the weapon. Then he withdrew his own life-taker and felled Tillman by smashing it's iron forcefully into his stomach.

"I've already told you, I'm not dying today," he declared as Tillman, unable to draw breath, writhed in agony at his feet. "But trouble me again and you will be."

Without casting any glances towards any of the distant onlookers, or the two women whose faces now peered out of Eduardo's window, the Outlaw swung himself casually onto the Arabian and heeled it in the direction of the lowering sun. Kneeling in the dirt, Tillman spat out a mouthful of sand and cursed at the dark figure in the distance, vowing to avenge his humiliation.

Chapter 7

Only a solitary shot had been fired by the Outlaw, and that veered deliberately high. He did not aim at the leader of the charging dozen or so vigilantes, and now he was at the mercy of their pointed rifles. He was sure of his aim, but he had decided today would be the beginning of the end of his journey.

How many more minutes of breathing in the hot sandy air were now in the judgment of the galloping bounty hunters? His hands were cramped with days of hard riding and his eyes gritty from the rising dust. He sighed, almost with relief, believing the end was inevitable.

He tossed his rifle to the ground and held his arms aloft as he wilfully and acceptingly submitted to his captors.

The sweaty, revengeful victors were jubilant and relieved that they had captured their man without endangering their lives. They circled the lone figure stood next to the exhausted Arabian, causing a swirling dust cloud which could be seen from miles around.

Sheriff Leighton Dykes, sworn in by Judge Bechstein to catch or kill the murderer, considered it dishonourable to shoot a yielded man. He also wanted to make an example of the Outlaw by sealing his doom legally after the quick deliberation of justice and law.

He knew thousands of spectators would gather at the famous hanging tree in Rio Rojo to witness the demise of the disgraced vermin.

He was pleased that his vigilantes had paid tribute to his orders not to shoot in the pursuit. The posse knew it was a strange request which defied Texas logic, but they understood his rules and they were fully aware this lawman from Austin demanded dignity and restraint from his accomplices.

In this rare breed of sheriff, he maintained it was the privilege of the law to decide who should live and die. He was a man who had trod lots of leather and ridden many miles. His loyalties were to the employers he served, to the law, and to God.

His resolution was to uphold the law and protect the weak. He was tough and uncompromising, built with stern principles that he would never betray for money or convenience.

Although the Outlaw was expecting a volley of lead to end his days, he did not care how he took his last breath.

Since leaving Rio Rojo three weeks ago, reflection and remorse had possessed his every thought. A great lamentation and sullen contemplation manifested within him again, as the souls he had dispatched to ride high in the clouds tormented his every thought and the ghosts of his bullets haunted his every dream.

The tiredness that began a long time ago now veiled over him, blocking out all solace. He no longer saw the leaves move in the breeze; he could not hear nature's chatter. No longer did he see the sunshine and the bright blue of the cloudless sky, and no longer did he notice filling his lungs with fresh pure air.

All he felt was emptiness and numbness. He was unable to refill his soul with any joy or purpose. He no longer held hope that life certainly led toward a light worth seeking. He was a shadow of his former being, with the lone road to Hell his only comfort.

He had seen the rising dust of the hunters from afar, but with every passing day the amusement of evasion dwindled until finally he sank into submissive surrender, relinquishing his rifle and his revered Tranter to the sheriff.

The descending prairie darkness forced Dykes to prematurely halt the posse's return to town and make camp. The mood around the huge dancing flames was jovial, and the sound of laughing and fiddle playing extended deep into the developing black expanse of nothingness.

The scent of roast meats and coffee wafted and tormented the hungry Outlaw. Tied to a tree at the very edge of the firelight, with his back to camp and facing the expansive prairie, he watched the huge sun sinking in the far distance. The crunch of dirt to his rear caused him to turn his head to the approaching steps.

"You know you and me got some strange similarities."

"Ya think?" The Outlaw did not look up at the approaching sheriff, who lowered down in front of his prisoner with a tin plate of charred meat and hot beans.

"Both plucky and courageous." The sheriff spooned a mouthful of food up to the Outlaw. "We just got a few different beliefs, that's all."

The sheriff did not feel sorry, nor hold any compassion for the bank robber; he simply had an appetite to understand what motivated someone with an opposite creed to his own. Equally pressing and important to the sheriff was finding out the Outlaw's name.

"I'd say there's a little more to it than just that," he answered, rolling the hot food around in his mouth. "Your code is not violence or villainy."

"Maybe, but one thing is for sure. We're both famed in our lines of work." Dykes scraped the fork across the tin to scoop more beans.

"You enjoy your work, sheriff." The Outlaw looked Dykes in the eye.

"Why hell. Yes, I do," he boasted a reply, wondering the reason for the question.

"Then there's one might difference right there. You see, I hate my achievements and I know there ain't any glories in them that make me proud," the Outlaw admitted.

"Yeah. I guess you ain't rightly made your mama too proud, have you boy?"

"She's unaware."

"That's why you keep your name secret, so you ain't embarrassing her none," he casually probed.

"No, it's just my way of keeping to minding my own business. That's all," he swallowed. "And besides, my mama's been sleeping a long time now."

"That so." Dykes tried to act nonchalant.

"It's just my way. Nobody needs to know my name." The Outlaw shook his head dismissively.

"Courtesy costs nothing, yet it is priceless?"

"It ain't going to change my passage none."

"You know the preacher will pray for the Lord's mercy."

"And?"

"He'll need to convey a Christian name to the Lord above," Dykes continued.

"There'll be no mercy." The Outlaw was aware of Dykes' intentions, but needing the food, he continued to stall.

"You planning on taking it to your grave?"

"That's my intentions," he opened his mouth to accept more food.

"It seems to me your craving for fame. Only to be famous, you need to be known by a name."

"I crave neither fame nor infamy."

"Don't you think the loved ones of the dead should know the name of the man who hurled them into misery?" Dykes scraped the food around on the plate, sensing his failure.

"I don't figure it matter none. They can still grieve knowing I'm burning in hell."

"Ain't you going to repent and ask for the Lord's mercy?" Now irritated, Dykes held the fork to the plate.

"Hell no. I chose to do devil's work because God turned me away," the Outlaw knew his nourishment was over.

"The devil give you a name?" Irked by his disappointment, Dykes tried one last time.

"No. Just my poor old mama, and she's taken it with her to the grave."

Dykes straightened himself and cast a glance in the same direction as the Outlaw, watching the giant sun's final vestige as it disappeared in the far distance.

He sighed. "Well, fella, the sun has sure gone down on you."

He scraped the food from the plate to deny the disobliging Outlaw any more of his hospitality. He shook his head and walked back to the comforting warmth of the campfire.

The Outlaw glanced along Main Street where the citizens of Rio Rojo had crowded to see him. Mostly women and children, in this war-ravaged town where all were accustomed to violence, blood feuds, hardships, murders, and hangings, but the unexpectedness of the Outlaw's capture spread fast throughout the desert towns, outposts, and homesteads, and all eyes looked on with fevered curiosity and, for a few, a soured disappointment.

There had been no shootout to the death, no end for the famed Outlaw in a blaze of glory which the gossipers and newspapers demanded, and being paraded into town as an exhibit was the harnessed mortal being.

People stood shoulder to shoulder and sought to gain an advantage of view by climbing high, standing on water barrels, peering out of windows, and scaling the rooftops to watch proceedings more comfortably.

The Outlaw, face shielded by the vaquero, looked ahead only, unconcerned and uninterested with all the attention. He passed by the hanging tree without even slanting a rueful glance.

A half-Indian girl leaned against a window on the first-floor veranda of Casa De Delicia and, looking down, she wondered what was causing the commotion on the normally deserted street.

The retired Gisty released a sardonic grin. "Why damn my eyes." He tipped his hat to acknowledge the supreme work of Sheriff Dykes as he rocked in his chair with his defunct foot raised and bandaged, then he scowled at the villain with contempt and condemnation.

An excited red hound, actively confused, leaped, barked, and ran eagerly back and forth, wondering if the hunt was over or just beginning until he was chased away by one of the swaggering captors.

A woman stepped down from the boardwalk and flung herself on the floor in front of the parade. From her knees she shouted incoherently and vindictively to the secured prisoner who had taken the life of her husband many years ago.

"May you roast in hell for what you did that day!" she scorned, insult after insult now he was not protected by his gun. "I hope you have a long and painful death." She berated his cold blood, his ancestors, and his origins, waving her arms frantically hoping to turn his fixed gaze.

His rigidity did not bait, and it was Leighton Dykes who twitched his fingers on the lock of his rifle to indicate to his second he had heard enough and it was time to remove the hysterical widow from in front of them.

The Outlaw ignored all the clamour and attention.

Even the tearful and handkerchief-waving Mattie Darell, who was mourning his capture along with her crutch-leaning son, could not rouse enough interest from the killer for him to cast a glance in their direction.

He was pleased the boy had survived the injury, but he did not acknowledge their lamentation as onwards towards Gisty's jail he stared, with the brim of the vaquero pulled low to prevent revealing his nonchalant expression.

"If you've got anybody to say goodbye to, now's your last chance." Dykes knew of the town's long-standing tradition of allowing condemned men one last opportunity to kiss his wife, children, or lover goodbye, and he held up the flat of his hand to stop the advance.

"Hellfire. You've got to be kidding me!" remonstrated Tillman, who had been idly leant on a hitch rail watching the exhibition swagger.

"This killer deserves no send-off," he shouted with rising concern.

"Traditions good as law round here, ain't it, soldier?" Dykes leaned forward across the horse's mane to face the soldier with the heavily bandaged hand who was making the objection.

"I'm the law in Rio Rojo," Tillman stepped to the edge of the boards drawing level with the fourteen horsemen.

"Not while I'm here," Dykes tapped a finger on the metal pinned to his chest.

"I wear the star and I enforce the regulations."

He then dropped his right hand down onto the handle of his pistol. "Now isn't it a tradition in these parts to permit a fella a send off before he faces his maker?" He shouted louder, looking left and right at the surrounding silent faces.

Tillman cussed and a conceited smile emerged as he shook his head slightly with a critical discernment.

For the first time, the Outlaw looked up and cast a sullen scowl across the mass of heads. No one moved, and no one spoke, no one offered to bid him a sympathetic good bye.

The unexpected question had stirred him for a brief moment and it touched him that from his abandoned boyhood and into the many years of his chosen profession, he had no companion or friend he could call to bid him farewell.

He knew if he mentioned the Darrells they would be ostracised and ruined before the day was done, so he too remained silent.

The Outlaw was a stranger known by no one, and he began to shake his head at the sheriff.

"Yes, it is." A woman shouted from behind the crowd of static bodies.

Gasps and sighs of disbelief sounded from all directions and the call was made again.

"Yes, it is tradition." She hollered again, but louder.

Heads turned in unison to the direction of the half Indian girl who was now stood between the door frame of the Casa De Delicia.

With the moment of loneliness being shattered, the Outlaw spun in his saddle to look down at the young smiling woman.

Dressed in a white, shoulderless, angelic dress which exposed the curves of her softness, her beauty captured his heart within an instant. The sheriff's forehead rutted; he recognised the look of mischievousness in the girl's eyes, but he could not understand the girl's reasoning for wanting to kiss his friendless captive.

"I'd like to say good bye to the dying man," she said with almost a musical tone, her teeth gleaming through a huge smile as she stepped away from the doorpost to the edge of the boards.

Twenty yards away on the other side of the street, Tillman spat angrily. "The hell you will." He then began to try and bustle his way through the numb and bewildered crowd as, at the same time, the astonished onlookers silently parted to allow Liberty May to stroll with languid grace towards the amused prisoner.

The Outlaw, posse, and sheriff gazed down at Liberty May's teasing approach, the generous curves of her sex exhibited proudly by the tight, low-cut dress which set perfectly upon her sensuous features.

Aubrey Willis had been watching the approach of the posse and the captured man from the comfort of his office window above Carlos's compound and tincture store. His jaw dropped and he spat out his half-chewed cigar when he saw the girl appear from the break in the crowd and outstretch her hand in the direction of the villain. His face mottled with rage and, tossing high the weekly accounts he had been scrutinising, he dashed towards the door.

A glow replaced the ashen mask on the doomed man as the colourful slender girl wiped her red lips with the back of her hand and reached up to place her warm hand upon his knuckles. She smiled again; the Outlaw suspected the confident smile was a perfected survival skill, but he mutually copied the cordiality.

"Can't a man hold a girl for one last time?" she said to the stone-faced sheriff, her voice pitching the sweetest melody to the Outlaw's ears.

Shocked by the girl's bold affront, he rocked slightly in the saddle and, after a considered lengthy pause, he nodded.

"Untie one hand."

Twelve pistols were drawn and pointed at the Outlaw as one of the posse moved in close to unfasten the binding that secured his hands to the pommel.

The girl held her breath as she looked into the face of the notorious killer.

The fine lines of lost youth on his face told of an infinite struggle and a shadow of recklessness, yet she saw intelligence and sensed a hidden deep humanity that had never been allowed to surface and nurture. Without a word being spoken, his grey eyes and valiant smile captivated her emotions and lured her senses. She had seen the wanted posters, read reports, and listened to the gossip and tales which romanced his handsome features; strikingly, she did not expect her emotions to be seized by an unforeseen and instant attraction.

Her intentions were driven by wanting only to cause a stir and ignite trouble between the three callous men in her life, Macklin Bucks, Charles Tillman, and Aubrey Willis, and not lose control of herself wildly in a hopeless situation with a man whose future consisted of only a date with the neck stretchers.

Again she wiped away lipstick and, with an agile spring, she placed her foot on his stirrup to bound up to his saddle. Landing on his lap, she threw her arms around his neck and pressed a kiss upon his lips.

He held the touch and responded by wrapping his free arm around the girl's shoulders. They remained locked for a long noiseless moment, the man on the threshold of death and the beautiful woman in the fullness of her youth, their misery connected in surprising equality of emotional warmth.

Some of the crowd laughed, some gasped, and others cussed at the audacious effrontery of the girl's act. The sheriff became agitated and the Outlaw momentarily forgot his ultimate fate.

The kiss lingered longer, much longer than everyone anticipated, and shocked and confused looks from the posse urged the sheriff to take action.

"Time's up!" he finally called. Annoyed and embarrassed by being ignored, he heeled his horse level to the Outlaw and reached across to pull the seductress's fixed arms away and break up the embrace.

Liberty May languidly slipped to the ground and it was she, not the Outlaw, who was now the focus of all eyes.

Moving back amongst the crowd with a lack of gracefulness, she looked back and asked:

"What's your name, mister?"

"He ain't known by a God-given Christian name, and he ain't ever going to be known by one either," bit back the annoyed Dykes before the Outlaw could open his mouth. "And there sure in hell won't be any remembrance on his grave marker!" he bellowed in recrimination at the girl.

The Outlaw continued to gaze and smile at the girl, neither knowing what to say nor how to say it, until his relished diversion was halted because Dykes noticed the switch in the crowd's attentions from the Outlaw to the girl and used it as an opportunity to move onward.

Rattling the reins, he hailed:

"Come on forward, let's go!" He nodded for the guard to refasten the hands of the Outlaw, then he added, "Move on… we're going to Austin."

Hesitation and looks of confusion amassed all around him as the riders and the Outlaw all wondered why they were riding out of town.

"Change of plan," he confirmed to the quizzical scowls. "We're going to Austin."

Sheriff Leighton Dykes had underestimated the interest in the capture of the Outlaw and, watching the size of the reception increase in both numbers and excitement, he feared a lynch mob would easily storm the door of the lock-up in Rio Rojo.

He eyed across the increasing gathering's restlessness, knowing they wanted to savour the Outlaw's death from the hanging tree, but to serve legal justice he knew the man's notoriety could only be preserved by the security only a fortified stronghold could provide.

With a "Yee haw!" he hurriedly heeled his horse and parted the crowd on the street to lead the posse out of Rio Rojo to the thunder of horse hooves.

Out of the mixed glares of disapproval and bemused hilarity appeared a stone-faced Tillman.

"You half-breed bitch!" he hollered, his cheeks purple with embarrassment. "How dare you embarrass me like this?"

"You leave this to me," ordered Willis, emerging from behind Liberty May. "You ain't thinking straight."

"Libby! You get back on up here, girl," shouted Daisy from the doorway of the Casa De Delicia. "Come on now. Back inside."

Tillman barged through the last of the silent, absorbed audience and swung his left fist across Liberty May's cheek. The force of the violence twisted Liberty's head sideways and thrust her body into the air. The thud of her uncontrolled fall made an imprint in the gritty sand and blood flowed from her slack mouth.

"Why, you low-down—" Before Willis had time to finish the slander, Tillman had reached across his body with his left hand and withdrawn his shooter to halt Willis's enraged approach with its aim.

Willis stopped, half-raised his hands to signal he was not armed nor prepared to fight, and tilted his head slightly to one side, displaying an uneasy smile. "We ain't exactly on equal terms here."

Enraged with anger and blazed humiliation, Tillman turned to the shock-still onlookers. "Throw him a gun!"

No one moved, and Tillman wildly and rapidly began to confront both men and women, screaming in their faces to toss Willis a gun.

Everyone hesitated, and no one acted to his command as he attempted to frisk for weapons with his bandaged hand. Instead of co-operating, the citizens of Rio Rojo slowly began to step back and distance themselves from the incensed captain to form a large circle around the scene of the injured woman.

Caught in a moment of insanity, Tillman continued his relentless frenzy until his eyes locked onto the thigh near to his right. In an instant, Tillman had seized the pistol and tossed it to the dirt at Willis's feet.

"Pick it up and preserve your claim."

Everyone knew Tillman's threat was directed towards their rivalry for the half-Indian, and, hoping to see at least one of the hated men squeeze on a trigger, they waited for bloodshed.

Tillman steadied his arm level. "Pick it up, you god-darn coward!"

Willis remained unmoved; his eyes flickered at the surrounding stares directed at him. His legs began to tremble and his lips quivered.

Tillman squeezed on the trigger, but the shrieks and scramble of bodies alerted him to the danger of many witnesses, and, casting an aggrieved scowl, he began to ease back his finger.

"You're not worth the god-darn lead," he said, and, with his anger yielding to sanity, he spun the pistol.

Then, beholding a look to confirm his dissatisfaction at the coward and the girl, he holstered the weapon, spat to the floor, and swivelled to elbow a passage through the silent throng.

"Holy Moses. That's gonna swell and bruise." Daisy rushed down from the whorehouse and knelt at Liberty's side. She carefully raised the unconscious girl's head to cradle it in her lap. "Come over here and help me get her inside," she called to the cowardly Willis.

Chapter 8

The posse sped over the dry, hard ground, their destination, Austin, was forty miles away. Here the Outlaw was to be expatriated for the many offences of which he had already been found guilty.

A cell of steel, a meal, and a noose awaited the man with no name.

They rode westerly with a breathless resolve, an urgency in which even the captive strangely abided. It was the hard riding that prevented the captors from noticing the extraordinary change that had taken place in the Outlaw since the episode of the kiss.

His flushing remained, burning away the cold mask of detachment, and his eyes were again alert, his lips wet and half open, as if the girl's kiss still lingered there. For the first time in his life, he had been possessed by a great passion that had not been stimulated by hate.

And it was the same urgency that made the riders careless, and, driving on and packing in tight around the Outlaw, they also failed to notice him working his hands free from the loose fastenings that once secured his hands to the pommel.

Back in Rio Rojo, when he was re-knotted after the kiss, the Outlaw had tensed up his muscles and swelled his wrists so that he could slowly work loose the binding as he was concealed by the mindless horde of riders that surrounded him.

The posse's way led through hard, dry grasslands which, in places, were hip deep with wild ferns and foliage whose tall palms brushed the horses' sides in their furious gallop and concealed the flapping of the captive's loosened braid.

The falling afternoon sun waned, a goldening on the residue dust cloud that the riders left on the brown and green scrubs as they sped across a vast open range.

In the distance birds sang, then fell silent, only to burst into song again as the vengeful storm of hooves rumbled past them on the hard dusty covering of soil.

The peaceful and serene landscape was more reminiscent of the natural prairie existence and half-sleeping herdsmen, rather than the devil dust of planned human sacrifice.

The glow of the sandy landscape began to dull as the sun sank lower and lower on the distant horizon, and, wanting to rid himself of the Outlaw as soon as he could and complete the journey to Austin without delay, Dykes informed the group he knew a watering hole just a few miles further which they would use to rest a while. Until then, he insisted the deliverance of the Outlaw must continue.

After a couple of miles of bounding over semi-dark barrenness, the group emerged on a large flat that sloped steeply down to a vast desert bowl of rock and grit.

As was the custom with excited cavalcades, they lost all dignity and control, and they raced at the steep drop at speed, accompanied with shouts and cries which heralded their arrival to all living beings within hearing distance. Heads arched low and facing forward, they were well underway when the Outlaw slipped his right hand from the bonds and grasped the reins from the hired man at his side.

Within an instant, the Outlaw had swung the Arabian and was heading up the steep incline, at an angle, his body being in full rhythmic cadence with each movement of his galloping horse.

Most of the posse continued on, unaware of the escapee, and herd-like they charged down the hill towards the plain at full speed. Only the sheriff and the guard who held the prisoner were aware of the bold, ambitious breakaway, and by the time they had pulled their mounts to a stop, the Outlaw had already covered fifty yards.

The sheriff's hopeful and aimlessly repeated gunfire from the confiscated Outlaw's Tranter alerted his small army, but the Outlaw was already at the top of the steep, gritty incline before they could safely pull to a halt and begin their turn.

The sheriff waved his arms hurriedly, signalling that he wanted his men to give chase, even though they all knew by the time they had made the steep climb the Outlaw would be a distant figure, soon to disappear in the rapidly descending dusk.

However, emboldened with fury, the sheriff gave orders to kill the fugitive at first sight and he led the hunt. He searched for over two hours until, with only the speckles of stars to break the sheer blackness, he struggled to trail the fugitive and eventually had to humiliatingly admit to his men the pursuit was over for the night.

Chapter 9

Leant across the supporting thigh of Daisy, Liberty May had managed to watch the convoy disappear and the fracas between Tillman and Willis through blurry eyes.

Her brief popularity had now passed. The outraged women who cussed at the Outlaw and wished him a painful end emerged from the surrounding onlookers and spat in the groggy girl's face.

"Shame on you!" Her venomous glare brought a queasy feeling and involuntary shivers to Liberty.

In a storm of hysterics, she continued to scream denunciation of the whole town and the witnesses who found momentary exultation from Liberty May's exhibition. Then she spat again. "Shame on you, heathen!"

The crowd of circling feet began to slowly shuffle and spread thin, with murmurings of mixed discontent, humour, and disbelief. Only a few children stayed to look down at the two women. Wide grins still displayed their admiration for the one who had dared beyond their wildest imaginations to canoodle with the famed man who was destined for the gallows.

Shaking her vision clear, Liberty May wiped away the mucus from her face and allowed herself to be raised by Daisy and the dumbfounded Willis.

He told Daisy he was going to take Liberty home and discuss the events with her stepfather, Mac Bucks.

Not looking forward to feeling the full wrath of the old man, Liberty argued to stay, but Daisy dared not oppose the already humiliated Willis, and so she helped the weak-legged and shaky girl up to Willis's engaging arm.

Liberty had no intention of listening to Willis moan and rage about his own trauma and the indignity she had forced upon him, and so as soon as the two-mile journey to West Valley Ranch began, she exaggerated and feigned her suffering so much that she began to lose consciousness and slip in and out of delirium.

All throughout the hurried and bumpy journey she could hear Willis nasally breathing with an accompaniment of deep sighs as he tortured himself over and over with the image of his prospective wife sitting on the lap of the Outlaw. With her arms wrapped around his noose-bound neck and their faces joined as one, the embrace seemed to last an eternity.

He relived the disgrace and pondered his future. The incident had provoked him to halt his solicitations and issue Macklin Bucks with an ultimatum.

Willis was still besotted with the half-Indian girl, and the incident had only increased his desire for her, even though his patience had been tested and his humiliation was almost too much for him to bear.

He wanted to be in full control of Liberty's destiny, and Mac must either accept his proposal of a marital union to his stepdaughter for the agreed substantial payments, or the petitioning was over.

Liberty ignored the waking calls and soft revival taps upon the unmarked side of her face. She kept her eyes firmly closed and muttered inaudible nonsense to avoid the questions and threats from her outraged stepfather as he and Willis hauled her limp body to her bedroom.

She could tell from his soft hands it was Willis who laid her head comfortably on the pillow, and equally she knew it was Mac who carelessly dropped her legs onto the mattress. With the door closing behind them, she could just hear the heated discussion continue beyond the door with unchaste comments of astonishment.

The debate moved into the living room, and engagement commenced regarding marriage. After a long period of muffled dialogue which Liberty could not decipher, she heard Willis shout from outside.

"I'm going to send for the doctor."

She leaped forwards and towards the window, where peering through the gap in the curtain she saw a smiling Willis wave back towards the doorway where she presumed Mac was returning the acknowledgement.

The men's parting seemed cordial, and she suspected the kiss had not damaged the relationship between Willis and her stepfather as she had hoped.

Moments later, hearing Mac's boots clamber the stairs, she pounced back into bed and closed her eyes. The door opened just enough for Mac to cast his bitter gaze at the girl. He cussed at her lunacy and the display which had almost destroyed his future, and he slammed the door against its frame.

An hour or so later the town's only and very old doctor paid a brief visit. Confusingly, he too found the girl unresponsive; however, unconcerned regarding her health, he soon left issuing her with a bottle of tincture and a scribbled invoice for his brief consultation.

Darkness soon descended as Liberty May slumbered in her room, her mind lambent with the images of the handsome Outlaw with the sunburnt face and bright eyes.

She had been kissed before, but not like this; they had either been forced or by chance. When she was younger she had played a game called "I'm-a-lip-in," where boys chased girls for a sweet kiss, and she had yielded in a sense of fair play to allow her predator the coveted prize. None of them felt like this; none of the kisses had caressed her heart and left her breathless. No man had attracted her before and tested the solace of her purity and innocence.

Her eyes fluttered, water spilled down her cheek, and her pulse raced uncontrollably. She had been kissed and captivated by a nameless man whom she did not know and a man she would never see again.

She wondered if he remembered her, and she cried into her pillow knowing that the brief passage could never be replicated, and nor would her senses feel more alive and invigorated than they did in that fleeting embrace.

Now lying on her bed she felt more alone than ever before, her heart beating loudly, knowing that it was no use trying to kiss or hold another man. She knew she would be just holding on to emptiness whilst thinking of the Outlaw and their last caress.

Raised voices from downstairs returned her thoughts to the present. She slid out of bed, deliberately walking over the crumpled harlot bodice, to squint towards the hitch rail in the yard where three militia men waited in their saddles; a fourth horse was riderless.

Liberty May now knew the debate from under the floorboards was between Mac and Tillman. She presumed he too had now ridden over to the West Valley Ranch to vent his exasperation and seek future assurances. She did not burden herself with the affair, and she stayed within her room where the words were indistinct.

She knew why Tillman was berating Mac, and she cared little. She blew out the solitary candle and slithered back into bed.

Her thoughts were for no one except the Outlaw. It was him and only him who concerned and distressed her.

Would he think of her in his last few moments, and if he did would his thoughts be of a crazy whore who was craving attention, or would he have seen beyond the gaudy outer garb to feel the tenderness of the girl's emotions and true longing?

Crying into the pillow with a racing heart, she knew she would never see the Outlaw again.

The disturbance below was short, and soon the thumping of departing horses followed by Mac bedding down for the night was all that could be heard.

Slowly she took to an uneasy slumber in a fearing, apprehensive silence that loomed over the West Valley homestead; she knew the short edgy peace would be ruined by Mac's fury when the first traces of the morning light revitalized the horizon.

The Outlaw didn't have to ride the Arabian hard to lose Sheriff Leighton Dykes and his posse. The risky but well-planned manoeuvre halfway down the hill gave him an advantage, and he knew his horsemanship would be more than equal to the posse.

Only the Arabian losing her footing on the hard rocks would enable the posse to catch up with him, and in the sheer blackness of the wilderness he knew Dykes would not be able to track his trail.

He ambled on slowly for another half dozen miles before deciding to rest on a small cluster of dense cedars which were situated on a high bank that dominated the dry expansive landscape, and where, come daylight, any rising horse dust would be seen easily.

With no food or water, there was little to do except rest and listen to the strange cries of birds echoing in the fluky dark and reminisce about the girl who had resurrected his being.

He could still smell her citrus freshness, feel the warmth of her breath, and the softness of her hair which had flickered in the breeze across his face.

He rested his eyelids and in the blackness he saw deep into her gaze, and he sensed a longing for help and a yearning for a returned desire. He shrugged off the vision, reasoning this was just the imagination of a tired man with a lost soul who had given up life's addictions for the reward of a noose.

He shook away the tiredness—not the tiredness which was fixed by sleep, but the tiredness which afflicted his energy for life. His spirit had been resurrected by the girl, her impulsiveness had touched his heart, and he believed her desire to be honest. The negative bleakness that plagued him was now lifted from within, and he felt a strange elation, a resurgence within his former being that fervently beat an unyielding craving to now live and seek out the girl who had ignited his desires.

He rested his head again, wondering what the girl was doing, where she lived, and if she had thoughts or dreams about him. He cared little for her profession or if she had ruined herself with a lurid reputation. He was well aware harsh times and a cruel existence had ensured many women stained their character with a will of desperation for survival, but he knew both their past immoralities could be erased if he returned for her.

Finally, as his lids bore down heavy on his eyes, a shimmer from within the foliage caught his eye.

At first he thought it was the twinkle of a night creature studying him from a distance; only the shine maintained a shimmer until a cloud obstructed the moon's glow and the glint vanished.

Curiosity roused the Outlaw to probe the undergrowth, and he gasped with shock when the mystery was solved.

Reaching down towards where the glimmer originated, the Outlaw quickly withdrew his stretching fingers when they landed on a bone.

Cautiously and instinctively he glanced in all directions before using his foot to trample and part the foliage until he revealed to the moonlight a partial skeleton dressed in ripped and tattered women's clothing.

Delicately he tugged at a ruffled skirt to ease the remains from under the shrubs.

The discovery confused the Outlaw, and for a moment he stood motionless, studying the morbid discovery.

In front of him, lying on the dirt, was a small skeleton still covered in a sequin-decorated dress. Remnants of thick red hair still clung to the skin-free skull, which was plugged in the eye socket with a solitary lead shot.

Kneeling with an uneasy inquisitiveness for a closer inspection, the Outlaw noticed a rip in the dress revealed a small purse that must have been hidden inside the woman's bodice.

Carefully he nipped the purse between his fingers and slid it out from between the garment and the bones, then holding it in the flat of his hand he studied the padded pouch momentarily before he twisted open the clasp to empty its contents into his palm. Dismissing crumpled notes and several items of finery, his attention was drawn to a large solitary jewelled necklace which he carefully raised high by its chain until it glinted a dark red cast from the luminescent naked moon.

He blew away dust and the necklace spun, flashing reflections of light that splice through the darkness. Curiously he stopped the rotating jewel and rubbed his thumb across the source of the sparkle to reveal ingeniously crafted glass-looking initials 'LM'.

Shaking his head with bewilderment, the Outlaw dropped the expensive piece into his inside pocket, but he sensed some compassion for the dead woman who must have deliberately concealed the purse, so he returned the rest of the items back into the purse and slid it attentively back within the framework of her bones.

Again he deliberated over the mauled and rotten body. He could see where scavenging prairie dogs had left their teeth marks scratched on her femur, and a pile of soil next to a shallow grave indicated carnivore diggings. Looking around in the semi-blackness, he could see no other clues to denote her demise or to why she was concealed with just a scattering of soil beneath the foliage.

With the remains still wearing what appeared to be evening wear, including ankle boots, and in the absence of a coffin and a decent burial, the Outlaw suspected wrongdoing. If the woman had been shot in the head and abandoned in a hurry as he believed, he could not understand why the murderer buried her whilst she was still decorated with her jewels. Dragging the bones back beneath the foliage and scattering dust over them with the side of his boot, the Outlaw decided that he could do no more for the woman and, now weary to the point that his thinking hurt his head and his eyes stung, he needed to rest.

Chapter 10

Liberty May didn't have to wait for the sun rise to wake her. She hadn't slept; her thoughts were plagued with the misery of not seeing the Outlaw again and the sorrow of him going to his grave without knowing her name. She had donned her usual brown Holland gown and got to work lighting the fire to cook Mac his breakfast. It wasn't long before the sizzle of bacon fat roused Mac as she had planned, but he saw straight through Liberty's charade.

"What's this I've been hearing about your doings in Rio?" he shouted, wiping the tiredness from his eyes. "Honey goglin' with an Outlaw."

"I reckon you heard it straight." Liberty did not raise her face from the direction of the hot pan.

"Of all the lowdown desperate tricks." He strode across the bare wooden floor. "The Outlaw!"

"If that's what they're calling it." Without the need to see Mac's body position, she braced herself.

"Why you no good little half breed bitch!"

The palm of his hand cracked hard against her cheek.

"What in the blazes you thinking of?"

He watched the power of the blow drop her to the floor.

"Being close to marriage an' all."

He did not help her to her feet.

"Darn fool... two men of prominence seeking to take you in... a lousy little half breed that no sane man will even look at and you go and canoodle with a murderer." He shook his head.

"Can't see much difference." She uttered into her hands which were soothing the slap burn.

Mac did not clearly hear the comment because of wood scraping as he dragged back a chair at the table.

"Are you unhinged?" He sighed as he dropped into the chair, then picking up a spoon he shouted, "Quit your carping and bring my breakfast. I don't want to hear another squaw word come out of your mouth."

Liberty May was oblivious to his words; her mind had drifted back to happier times when she was hand in hand with her mother. Life was peaceful, free spirited, and uncomplicated.

"I bet the whole god damned town is talking. Made a fool out of all of us."

Stretching out her arm to keep as much distance between them as possible, she carefully placed Mac's breakfast in front of him.

"I need to figure how we're going to get out of this stink."

He grabbed a slice of cornbread and tore it into two pieces to soak in the hot fat.

"I blame that haughty sheriff they called in. Thinking he was doing all right and legal by taking him into Austin when they shoulda just strung him up from the hanging tree and plugged him full of lead whilst his neck was still stretching."

He paused his grumbling to chew on a piece of bacon. "But no. He wanted to play the high and mighty law pleaser."

Liberty had turned her face to the window. The morning sun warmed her face and, for a while, she was oblivious to his comments until he added,

"Well I guess it doesn't matter so much anyways. His neck will be stretching long round about now."

She looked at the few lingering clouds high on the horizon, her eyes hoping to glimpse a divine sign or spiritual message just as she did as child when one of the tribe's elders had departed for another world.

Seeing nothing except bright blue dappled with pure white and wanting to avoid more castigation, she quietly headed back to her room. She saw the bruising left by Tillman and the reddened palm mark from Mac as she passed by the hall mirror.

She needed to occupy her mind and rid herself of thoughts of the dead outlaw so she could concentrate in full and plan how she would break free from the grip of the three men and make her escape from La Vaca County.

Feathering the swelling with her fingers, she vowed silently that she would be damned in hell before she would wed either Aubrey Willis or Charles Tillman.

Quickly she made her bed and folded away the bawdy garments which lay still crumpled in the corner where she threw them, then sitting on the bed in languid contemplation, she kept an alert ear to Mac's activities down stairs.

She heard him finish up in the kitchen, pull on his boots, and check his rifle, as was his daily routine when he went out to feed his few remaining livestock. However, today's regime was conducted with cussing expletives regarding Liberty's senseless actions, her careless attitude, and her bloodline.

Slamming the door behind him, he looked up at her window and raised his rifle in her direction and ordered Liberty not to leave the house for any reason. She smiled, mainly to annoy him, knowing his threat was a bluff. He could bully and beat her, but she knew her life was too valuable to him for it to be wasted by lead. He stomped across the yard, glancing in all directions, his mind occupied. The bareness of the barn confirmed he was not yet ready to stop receiving the benefits from Willis's and Tillman's wooing, although he was inclined to conclude the matter before the end of the night and before any type of misalliance made Liberty May unbefitting or ineligible for wedlock. He begrudgingly admitted that tonight he would not be driving Liberty to Casa De Delicia in quest for a few extra dollars for fear of jeopardising his future rewards.

After only a few minutes Liberty heard the main door swing open. She thought he had returned to check she had not fled.

"Libby! Libby!" Mac hollered from the doorway. She swung her feet from the bed; she had not reached the door before he called out again.

"Libby. Where in darnation are you, girl?"

"I'm coming," she replied, reaching the stairwell.

"You hear anything last night?" She was unsure what to reply.

"You hear anything?" he repeated.

She wondered if he was testing her to find out if she had heard anything from Willis or Tillman which may give her reason to flee.

"Well! You deaf now?" He looked up at her stationary figure. "You see anybody?"

"What?" she grimaced, expecting another berating.

"You see anybody outside?"

"Aubrey Willis, but he was with you," she decided to be honest.

"See anybody else? Hear anybody else?" His face displayed urgency.

"Yes, I saw Charles Tillman and his cronies come by later."

"Anybody else? Over by the pasture?" He pointed over his shoulder with his thumb.

"No. No one. After Tillman left I heard nothing."

"Erm. You sure, because there's god darn tracks out on the pasture and they sure aren't mine." He wrapped his gun belt around his waist and buckled it tight.

"Go and saddle Bowie," he instructed her, preparing his favorite horse as he stocked his pistol with ammunition.

Liberty May hurried across the yard towards the stable. She glanced to the pasture on her left. The shallow incline of wild grassland led through to a dense thicket of redbuds and desert willows which provided the perfect secluded vantage point to watch the homestead from a distance.

Mac met Liberty May outside the barn as she led out the chestnut quarter horse.

"God darn blue bellies are doing a recon for easy pickings," he cussed as he hauled himself up to swing into the saddle. "Well, I'll show the sons of bitches! Thinking they can pussyfoot in here and help their thriving hands to my stock."

"What are you going to do?"

"Track the skunks, and when I find out where they're camped up I'll swing on by Tillman's and chase 'em all back over the canyon with their tails between their legs and with lead up their asses."

"Well, be careful." Liberty hoped he wouldn't make it back. Mac didn't reply as he heeled Bowie into motion. He knew the comment lacked any sincerity.

Liberty May deliberated her future just as she did every day when she harboured endless thoughts of running away and escaping from West Valley Ranch and La Vaca County, even though she knew her prospects of survival away from Rio Rojo would be bleak.

If she did manage to escape the pursuit of Mac and Tillman, the chances of her finding a sympathetic saviour who would treat the Texas mud blood with any affection and sincerity would surely be impossible.

Only desperate men like Tillman and Willis would offer her any existence, and she ended her deliberation with the same conclusion as she always did: stay and face the prospect of a miserable life with either Willis or Tillman and pray that God would call them early and leave her with their wealth.

Returning to the homestead with a gallop, Mac's ashen face revealed concern.

"Yankees?" Liberty met him in the yard and took the reins.

Throwing himself from the saddle he ordered, "Tend to Bowie."

Liberty knew the anger in Mac's eyes was not ignited by thieving soldiers.

"Did you follow the trail?" she persisted.

"None of your concern."

He marched towards the house, his mind occupied with a trail which led him to Aubrey Willis's cabin.

It was Willis who had been spying on the household from the safety of the pasture, and Mac knew he would have seen Tillman's arrival later that evening.

Rage pulsed through his veins and choked all of his reasoning. Now Mac wanted to dig in his heels and prove to Willis he would not be rushed or pressured into selling off his stepdaughter without receiving her full worth.

He had made up his mind; he was going to force both Willis and Tillman to increase their generosity one last time.

"When you've finished in the barn get yourself washed up n'all fresh for tonight," he shouted over his shoulder. "The posse will be riding back in from Austin."

He knew these wild men would lose control of their enhanced finances now their duty was done and the reward money collected. Their spirits were sure to be high after completing their daunting duty.

"I want to be in Rio before sundown. Catch the early burners before they hunker on down."

Liberty May dawdled with her duties and hesitated returning to the house. Over and over she brushed down Bowie until his dark mane and chestnut coat reflected from the bright shafts of the low afternoon sun which pierced through the gaping barn slats.

She heard the approaching tread of leather on the grit outside and braced herself with monolithic hardness.

"What the hell's taking you so long?"

The door swung open and she squinted at the man with his belt wrapped around his hand and its tail hanging loose by his side. Liberty May shuddered under her wrap.

"Get yourself ready for work and be quick about it," he pounded his feet forward. "You know I wanted an early start tonight."

She ignored his bellowing and, facing Bowie, she slowly continued the stroke of his mane knowing full well her disobedience would enrage Mac further.

The crack of leather across her back forced her to drop the brush and scream out in pain. She collapsed into the straw, just avoiding the stomping hooves of the startled horse which squealed, reared up, and pulled away to the back of the barn.

"Lazy bitch!" Mac reached down and grabbed her plaited hair and began to drag her out of the barn. "You need to start paying for your keep, you no good half breed."

Stumbling to her feet and fending off his hand from her hair, Liberty allowed Mac to haul her by her arm into the house, up the stairs, and to the bedroom where he barged her through the doorway and threw her on top of the folded night costume.

"You've got five minutes!" he threatened, swinging the belt across her back again. "I'll be out front with the cart."

He then slammed the door behind him and pounded down the steps. "Don't make me come and find you again."

Hearing the house door slam, Liberty May's body began to shake feverishly in a spasm of weakness and shock. She cried loudly, releasing tears into her cupped hands.

Her emotions controlled her breathing and she panted rapidly to fill her lungs. Finally she tentatively touched her sore scalp and ran her fingers through her bedraggled hair. Blood dripped on her fingers and began to trickle down her neck.

She rested her palm on the side of her waist where her burning skin swelled and she winced, throwing herself face down in the pillow to try and subdue the pain.

After a few minutes, she heard Mac positioning the cart outside and his throaty horse command jolted her from the agony.

She drew in a long deep breath, held it, and tensed her body. Closing her eyes and gritting her teeth hard, she decided in that instant her future.

Instead of brooding, a wild surge of determination and resolution had composed her. She had made up her mind that tonight she would steal a client's gun and shoot Macklin Bucks dead.

If anyone interfered, they too would meet the same fate. She had changed her mind and decided that she would rather face the future of a noose rather than a life of toil and punishment with either Aubrey Willis or Charles Tillman. She drew in another becalming breath and arose from the bed.

Chapter 11

The sun had fallen below the horizon as Mac's cart straightened onto Main Street. Lanterns swung and window candles cast a faint orange across the boardwalks, intermittently breaking the blackness of this yet starless night.

The normal evening silence and desolation in Rio Rojo had not been replaced by rowdy celebrations as Mac had hoped.

Posse horses were hitched on the rail outside Eduardo's, but only muffled voices could be heard, not the raucous celebrations he expected.

A momentary flash of light beamed across the dirt in front of Mac and Liberty as two men barged out of the saloon door. Wrapping their arms around each other, they fell to the floor.

Mac and Liberty could hear both men blaming each other for being bone-headed loafers, and they cussed and swore as they rolled, kicked, punched, wrestled, and spat at each other, until, stepping out from the darkness, Sheriff Leighton Dykes pulled back the triggers on both of his pistols and pressed the barrels into the cheeks of both men.

Mac and Liberty could not hear Dykes' sobering threat, but his actions had the desired effect, and both men quickly dusted themselves down and scampered in opposite directions.

Dykes cast a glance towards the stationary cart and holstered his weapons, then with an acknowledging nod he turned his back and disappeared inside Eduardo's tequila hut.

"Get out and go to work." Those were the first words exchanged between Mac and Liberty since they left the ranch over one hour ago. "And no funny business," he warned. "I'll be over to check on you, so make sure you put on a big nice welcoming smile for the fella's." He raised his hand to her face and forced her lips to curl with his thumb and finger. "Now go and git."

He then pressed against her shoulder with force to urge her from the cart, and once she had stepped down, he yelled at the horse to move on towards the corral.

"Back again?" said Daisy, her surly face unimpressed.

She did not want the squaw girl who kissed the famous hanged man to dissuade any drunk men from entering the establishment. "I'm surprised to see you're still in one piece."

"He wants… err… needs me to turn a dollar or two."

"Well, I doubt that's gonna happen any time soon." Daisy looked over her shoulder and pointed to the rear of the building. "Go and make yourself comfortable in the back of the parlour and keep out of the way of speculators."

Daisy knew men with little funds often peeped through the door to glimpse the sultry half-dressed tantalising women.

By keeping Liberty out of their sight she could ensure other prospecting visitors remained oblivious to the girl's presence, whilst preventing the peepers of spreading distasteful gossip of her presence in the bordello.

"And don't come out or say anything unless I come and get you."

Daisy dictated Liberty's movements by clasping her hand tight around her forearm, and she ushered her past the arrangement of chaises and highly polished mirrored furniture to the dimly lit rear.

Mac stood in the open doorway of Eduardo's and gazed at the lethargic and muted collection of gunmen. The scene was not as he expected, and he sensed the men were not celebrating liberally for a posse who had just delivered Texas's most wanted man to the grave.

Three men stood at the bar quietly chatting, four were dourly playing cards without any gusto, whilst two others semi-dozed in high-backed chairs.

Alone at the far end of the bar, with his head drooped and staring blankly at his empty whiskey bottle, Sheriff Dykes' attention was drawn to a steep slope twenty-five miles west.

"Buy you a drink?" Mac offered as he neared the bar. "Say, can I buy you a drink?" he repeated to the unresponsive lawman.

"Uhh... sorry."

"I'd like to join you for a drink," Mac said again.

"I don't want to insult you, friend, but I'm not inclined for company right now." The sheriff did not break his gaze from the empty bottle.

"Ah come on. This is empty." Mac grabbed the bottle by its neck and waved it towards the tender. "Let me buy you a fresh one to celebrate."

"Celebrate what?" Still, the sheriff avoided eye contact.

"Celebrate what?" Mac repeated. "You kidding me?"

He reached out and took hold of the new bottle as the barman slid across another glass.

"Taking that vermin into Austin for his neck pulling."

He plucked out the cork with his teeth. "That's worth celebrating." He spat the cork and began to fill the first glass.

"There'll be no celebrating." Dykes levelled his hand across the top of his glass. "Not tonight."

He released a brooding smile and shook his head. "Not by any of the law-standing folks around here, that is."

Then he raised his head and swivelled to turn his shoulders. "You see, these useless sons of bitches let him loose." He shouted loud enough for all to hear.

"What?" Mac muttered as the sheriff grabbed the bottle and threw it against the far beams. All conversations immediately stopped as glass and whiskey sprayed in all directions.

"Incompetent fools took their eyes off him."

All heads turned in Dykes' direction.

"Can't just blame us, boss," one of the card players defended.

"Yeah, it was your idea to take him to Austin," backed up another man through the haze of tobacco smoke.

Mac shrugged in astonishment and leered at the sheriff. Respected throughout all of Texas for his mastery and hired by Judge Bechstein for his fastidious consummation of all things legal, Mac struggled to understand the sheriff's misfortune.

"Yeah, we'd have much just strung him up from the hanging tree." Mac saw Dykes' eyes widen and his lips narrow.

"You no-good cattle herders!" he shouted, withdrawing his pistol and firing off lead into the wood above. "Get out of my sight... the lot of you!"

Only the two men who were dozing moved; the deafening blast jolted them and caused them to douse themselves in their unfinished drinks.

The sheriff fired again and repeated. "Go get. I don't want to see any of your miserable ass'd faces again tonight." More splinters fell and fluttered in the gun smoke. "You lot couldn't track a three-legged coyote."

He stretched out his pistol-wielding arm again, but this time chairs and stools were knocked over as the men hurriedly grabbed their drinks, collected their hats, and scrambled towards the doorway.

Mac saw the opportunity to steer some trade towards Daisy's place and he dropped his hand on the shoulder of one of the fleeing men to suggest, "Why don't you fella's finish up over the road?"

"You crazy? We didn't get paid." The bearded man paused and struck a look of resentment at Mac. "We ain't got no money to spend on whores."

"I heard that outlaw's girl is sitting all comfy over there," Mac tried to set thoughts of reprisal into the man's anger. "You could take your revenge out on her."

The crewman did not hear Mac's last words. He had dismissed his suggestion, and he neared the door with haste.

Mac saw Dykes smile and he wondered why.

Chapter 12

"Where's that little Indian bitch?" The door of the Casa De Delicia swung inwards with force, startling the scantily dressed prostitutes and shattering the serenity.

"You know the rules, sheriff." Daisy put down her drink and arose to face the swaying man in the doorway. "No guns, no drinks, and no drunks."

"I'm not here to be lectured in profanity," he slurred his reply, slamming the door with his heel to confirm his intentions. He held up a whiskey bottle to his mouth and gulped until the last droplets dribbled onto his grey, stubbled chin. Then he staggered forward until he was halted by Daisy's half-bare chest.

The strong aroma of desert sage filled his nostrils, and Daisy's large, fleshy bosom occupied his view.

"Where is she?" He drooled, prising away his gaze to scan the room.

"Not tonight, sheriff."

Daisy held a firm stance to prevent him from walking any further.

"Bring out that squaw bitch." His eyes rolled across the heavily painted faces of the other Lolitas.

"She's not obliging tonight."

"I know different."

The episode with the kiss had rankled him, and his failure to deliver the captive brought humiliation upon him. He was a broken man now, bereft of any principles and morals. He had listened to Mac's devilment in the saloon and accepted the perverse, tempting poison which impelled him to gain personal revenge by satisfying himself with the Outlaw's girl.

"Not tonight." Daisy obstructed his path.

"Get out of my way, you lying bitch."

Now the stench of alcohol polluted the parlour and dominated the sweetness of the whores' homemade fragrances.

"Get her out here." She defied his insult and stood firm.

Dykes leant forwards, pushing his frame against Daisy. "Out of my way." His red-veined eyes penetrated deep into her unyielding and stern visage. "And now!"

Spittle caused Daisy to arch backwards, and the tone of the shout caused the girls to cower, some latching their arms around one another for comfort and support.

"I said—" Daisy did not finish her sentence.

The sheriff swung the empty bottle with speed against the side of her head. Daisy's back rebounded off the wall and crashed to the floor, taking with her a tall corbel planter.

Leaves, soil, and blood, with an accompaniment of screams, splattered an emerald green chaise.

He swayed over the semi-conscious female, sagging his head to the left and then to the right. He squinted to focus on the shocked whores who pressed themselves against the rear wall, then he withdrew the Outlaw's Tranter.

"Where's the squaw?" He threw his head back and slurred loudly in their direction.

No one answered.

He straightened his arm in the direction of Daisy and pulled back the hammer, then warned, "I won't be asking again."

Daisy's eyes widened, but she was too pained and disorientated to summon a reply. Dykes forced himself stiff to firm his aim and tease the trigger. Terror seized the whores, making them powerless to act, and losing all control of their nerves they clasped their hands over their faces to block out the vision and hide their fear.

"I'm here!" Thunder bellowed, and flame and smoke exploded to sting everyone's eyes.

Appearing out of the black smoke, Liberty May walked out from the shadows at the rear of the parlour, and Dykes smiled.

Daisy rolled over onto her side, her eyes level with the bullet hole in the timber floor; her breathing faltered and she fainted.

"Well, well. Lookisee here." Dykes grinned and holstered his gun. There she stood trembling in all her sullied resplendence, and now she was going to feel the power of his loins.

Wrenching his arm tightly around Liberty's waist as though he was collecting a prize, his legs defied him, and holding on to her for support he grinned and pointed towards the stairs.

Held vice-tight, Liberty's left arm was trapped between their swaying bodies. She reached down for his pistol and stretched out to extend her fingers, only to brush them across the walnut handle of his pistol. Several times she reached to grab the gun, but Dykes staggered, causing her grasp to fall short each time.

He shouldered and bounced off two room doors, which were locked each time, cussing. Eventually he barged his way through the door to room number three, which was at the end of the narrow, dimly lit corridor.

He pushed Liberty over to the bed with him as he stumbled, but she quickly composed herself and moved towards the small plain dressing table, which was positioned square to the room's only window.

With shaky fingers she lit an oil lamp; its flame turned blue as it billowed, and she poured water into a bowl to stall as she gathered her thoughts.

She gazed at her reflection in the black glass and a solitary tear dripped down her cheek.

Lowering her head she sighed, then drawing in a composed breath she raised her head again to the window to see the blurry reflection of Dykes removing his gun belt.

She held the gaze and her breath as she watched him struggle to unbuckle the leather.

"Help me get out of these god-darn boots," he ordered, slouching backwards on the mattress as he tossed the gun belt over the bedpost near his feet.

"Be right over." As her voice quivered, her eyes locked on the holstered weapon and her determination to get the gun strengthened. Now was the opportunity she craved, and she closed her eyes to block out any lingering doubts and plan the next move.

Stroking her hair to feign enticement, she made her mind up to lure Dykes into a lust-crazed daze and just when he had lost all control of his abilities she would lunge for the pistol and shoot him dead. She imagined every detail rapidly, over and over.

"What the hell are you waiting for?" Dykes ended her deliberation.

"I'm not paying for you to shine your tresses."

Liberty opened her eyes and braced herself. She knew it was now time to act, but as she began to turn, something beyond the glass caught her attention.

In the darkness outside she saw the stationary figure of a man. She paused and held her movement, squinted and focused hard at the shadowy figure, leant against the huge tree no more than twenty yards away.

Her eyes widened, her jaw gaped, and she released an uncontrollable gasp as a cloud drifted and the silver moon glow shone upon his face.

The Outlaw raised his head in her direction and smiled. She squinted again and shook her head to dismiss the apparition of the ghost, but the Outlaw remained in full view.

"Am I going to have to come over there?" Dykes threatened impatiently.

The distracting call prompted her eyes to fleetingly switch to the reflection at her rear, and when she looked back outside towards the tree, the man was gone.

Her eyes began to fill with water, and she had to knuckle away the tears to look again in the direction of the tree. She released another despairing sigh, accepting her mind was cruelly deceiving her.

"Well!" This time Dykes began to raise his body from the mattress.

Again Liberty drew another composing breath and braced herself. Gripping her hands into tight balls, she turned, but as she did she could not prevent herself from swivelling her head back to the window for one final and hopeful glance towards the tree.

Dykes dropped his leg over her lap and lay down as she tentatively sat on the edge of the rancid mattress.

With her eyes noting the exact position of the gun belt, she cupped the muddy, worn heel, pulled and tugged hard until she eventually slid the boot free.

She turned away, screwed up her face with a scowl of repulsion, and held her breath as weeks of travel fouled the air.

Dykes exhaled a long, relieving murmur and switched legs so his other foot could be relieved.

After the clumsy removal of the other boot, he pulled Liberty towards him, clutching tight her petite frame against his sweaty bulk.

He slobbered in her neck with his whiskey breath. "Now don't you be teasing me none." Then he whispered commands for her to remove her petticoat.

She gipped and began to struggle against his lusty advances; however, she did not possess the strength to resist the struggle, and inside she knew she did not have the fortitude to kill the man.

He sensed her disobedience and then felt her resistance. "Don't you go all cold on me now."

He pulled her close again and cupped her breast with his free hand.

"No!" she screamed.

Her resilience had failed her, and her emotions defied her. She despaired, knowing her plan had failed, and she pulled away.

She had hated the thought of killing him, but equally she hated his perverse touch. She screamed again, and as she did so the palm of his right hand crashed forcibly against the side of her cheek, turning her head sideways.

"Lousy bitch." He grabbed her by the throat and squeezed. "Don't want to play, uh!"

He released one hand to deliver another timed slap, then another, with enough force to spiral her away from him and across the bed.

Liberty May screamed, but through her blurred vision she saw the gun belt hanging over the bedpost near her. She rolled over and stretched out in desperation, but Dykes caught the reaching hand and tossed her over onto her back.

"God damn squaw!"

He pressed her body down against the mattress and hoisted himself on top of her. Drool fell from his loose mouth onto her face.

"Want to be treated like a savage, do you?"

He held her shoulders firm with his knees, and he secured her arms above her head with his enormous right hand and its powerful grip.

A psychotic grin emerged on his reddening face, and he began to tear at her clothing.

Her frailty was no match against his brutality, and he easily held her firm against the constant struggle.

"Makes no difference to me." He wetted his lips with his tongue and dropped his face into her neck to press his lips on her clammy skin.

She kicked her legs and frantically struggled to unseat him from her stomach, but his weight held her down as he barbarically continued to seek satisfaction. Writhing in desperation, Liberty May opened her mouth wide and lunged her head forward until she locked her teeth on his chin. Instantly he screamed, and he tried to pull away, but she held the bite until her mouth filled with his hot blood and she began to choke.

"You whore bitch!" With bulging eyes, he yelled whilst pressing the flat of his hand on the puncture. "I'm going to make you really wish you hadn't done that."

His knuckles smashed hard against her jaw, and all her resistance sapped as she submitted to an involuntary daze.

Dykes felt the teeth marks on his throbbing chin with his calloused fingers, then with incensed malice he tore open her bodice.

"You need lessons in how to treat—"

Dykes did not finish his words, as a sudden eruption of noise, blood, and brains instantly sagged his limp body.

Through the swirling gun smoke, Liberty saw a hand reach down, seize the collar of Dykes's corpse, and drag it off her.

Through her tears and smoke-smarting eyes, the face of the Outlaw emerged in front of her.

He lowered himself next to her and wiped away the dead man's dripping blood from her face with the bed sheet, then he wrapped his arm around her shoulder, firmed the support, and slowly eased her upwards to sit next to him.

He gently kissed her on the forehead, and she responded by wrapping her arms around his back and locking them into a lasting embrace.

No words were spoken as the pair hugged tight, losing themselves in a surreal and silent delirium.

Muffled voices of concern could be heard from downstairs, where scared whores speculated that Dykes had shot Liberty May.

The Outlaw broke the hold and gazed at Liberty from arm's length.

"I've got to get out of here."

He cast a quick scowl at the blood-squirting body, then, with a welcoming smile for his returning Tranter, he fastened the sheriff's gun belt around his waist.

He slanted his head towards the door where he heard the sound of creaking. He held his poise momentarily as he checked the bullet chamber in the smoking Tranter.

Firming his grip in his right hand, he quietly listened to clumsy steps and the whispers of the approaching curious as they assembled in the corridor.

He raised one finger to his lips, signifying he wanted Liberty to remain silent, then carefully wrapping his fingers tight on the door handle, he pulled the door inwards to reveal four wide, startled eyes.

Uncontrolled high-pitched screams were released by two whores who had crept along the corridor to investigate the sound of the gunshot.

The sudden door opening and the reveal of the dead sheriff and the pistol-wielding outlaw panicked the women into turning to flee.

With terror flooding their minds, they bumped into each other and bounced off the walls as they screamed incessantly and waved their hands in the air, as fear and shock dictated their quivering movements.

The Outlaw's eyes shone in the hue of the oil lamp, and he released a mirthful smile as he turned back to look at Liberty.

"Now it's definitely time I got out of here."

He listened to the screaming women and their heavy, graceless footsteps leave the building and echo down Main Street, then he holstered the Tranter and returned to Liberty May.

Even though her blood-stained and tear-damp face portrayed a mask equal to Dykes' death scowl, her beauty still stalled him.

"Others will have heard the shot." He neared the bed and arched over her. "And the screams."

Tenderly, he lifted her blood-splattered hair from her face and rested it behind her ears. "Will you come with me?"

He stretched out his hand, hoping for and anticipating her agreement, and his concerned frown swiftly disappeared into another smile as, without hesitation, Liberty's hand met and clasped his reach.

With ease, he raised her from the mattress and, continuing the motion, swung his arm under her buttocks to swoop her up into his arms and stride out of the doorway and into the dimly lit corridor.

Reaching the last step, which opened up to the deserted parlour, Liberty sobbed.

"Wait."

Her eyes had glimpsed a leg which extended out from behind tumbled furniture.

The Outlaw slid away his arm and guided Liberty May's unsteady feet to the ground, then guided her through the disorderly furnishings, which had been ruined in the panic, until they reached the semi-conscious madam.

They both knelt and Liberty cradled and tilted Daisy's head. Blood trickled from the strike mark and her eyes rolled white.

Releasing a pained gasp, she muttered, "Help me… please help me."

The Outlaw rested his hand on Liberty's forearm. "We've got to get out of here," and he shook his head slightly to show his concern.

"I can't just leave her like this."

Liberty grabbed a fallen bottle of whisky. "She's hurt."

She ripped the corner of Daisy's petticoat and poured the alcohol over it.

"Libby, is that you, Libby?" Daisy wallowed in delirium.

"You don't owe her." The Outlaw's brow furrowed. "She's not your boss now."

"No, it's not like that."

Liberty crumpled the cloth into a tight ball and released droplets of whisky over the laceration.

Daisy groaned. "I thought he had killed you."

She then murmured something inaudible and her eyes closed.

"I'm not what you're thinking." Liberty raised her face towards the Outlaw and looked him directly in the eye.

"Right now the only thing I'm thinking about is getting out of here." He heard the clamour from beyond the main door. "I don't care about your past, I just care about our future."

"I'm sorry, but I just can't leave her like this."

She gently patted the wound and Daisy winced as the cleanser stung.

"Someone will come and help her." He broke away from the incisive stare and straightened to look over his shoulder towards the door, where the noise of boisterous claims of retribution and justice were being made.

"I'm sorry," she sighed, placing her palm on the back of his hand.

"Then you will soon be cradling me in your arms." He withdrew the Tranter and levelled it at the door.

"No! You should go," she shouted.

"I'm not leaving you."

"You must!"

She propped a cushion under Daisy's head and stood with her back to the door. Daisy groaned, sensing Liberty had abandoned her, and intermittently roused from unconsciousness.

"I can't and I won't." He dropped his eyes from the door to look at her again. "I've been searching for you my whole life, and I'm never going to leave you." He feared his time with the girl he barely knew was almost at an end.

"You must." She grabbed his hand and cupped it with hers and kissed his skin.

"Leave now while you can." "Come with me," he implored as the gathering presence beyond the door increased.

He did not fear for his life; his only concern was that the girl did not reciprocate his feelings for her.

"Go with him." Daisy lifted her head and grimaced.

"No. I won't leave you." Liberty placed her palm on Daisy's cheek. "Not like this." Then she slanted a fretful smile towards the Outlaw. "Come back for me."

"What?" He heard her plea and returned a bewildered expression.

"I can't just leave this way." She shook her head and tears fell.

"Someone will take care of her." He was confused.

"I need to get some things from home." She stepped forward to lead him by the hand towards a rear window.

He turned away from the window to embrace Liberty again. "You won't need anything. I've got enough money hidden away to buy you everything you'll ever need."

"Come and get me later tonight." She hurriedly kissed him on the cheek and urged him, using her hands, to climb through the open window. "West Valley ranch… four miles south. Wait for me by the pasture on the bank."

Gently she pushed him away from the window and into the darkness of the rear yard, then pulled down the frame.

Turning back to attend to Daisy, Liberty heard a tap on the pane. She spun to see the Outlaw's smiling face close to the glass. He was holding up, to the light, a glistening gold and garnet pendant.

Liberty returned a pleasing but concerned smile and, knowing he would not leave until she had taken the offering, she quickly raised the glass and leant forward to allow his outstretched hands to lift the long wavy ringlets that cascaded around her bare shoulders and place the chain around her neck. In return, Liberty placed a gentle kiss on his cheek, then with a stern but kind-hearted abruptness she pushed him back into the blackness and slammed the window closed as a mass of pistols and rifles, all ready to release their malice, burst into the parlour and pointed in the women's direction.

"He's upstairs!" cried a semi-conscious Daisy, raising a finger towards the ceiling.

Chapter 13

Lurking in the shadows of the trees at the rear of the whorehouse, Willis watched the Outlaw climb out of the rear window only to change his mind and return a few seconds later.

Willis had chanced upon the Outlaw's escape, having found only frustration and increased concerns from his stakeout at West Valley, where he had watched Mac double-crossing him with Tillman. Pent up with anger and resentment by the lack of a firm agreement with Mac for Liberty May's hand in marriage, Willis had decided to watch over Liberty and Mac's affairs with Tillman from a distance. He had been spying on Liberty when the sudden appearance of the Outlaw shocked him. At first, he stepped back into the sheer blackness of a lean-to, but when the Outlaw reappeared to return to the window, he found himself tempted to grasp fame and adulation throughout the entire state. He primed his fingers and clawed at his pistol handle, but upon unholstering the weapon and levelling his arm in the direction of the unsuspecting man, his courage betrayed him. Stepping out from the crude shelter, his legs began to shake, his hand to tremble, and his lips to quiver.

He tried in vain to brace himself and tauten his muscles, but fear of failure and guaranteed death crushed him.

Still, he bit his teeth hard and squinted along his arm and barrel at the shadowy figure next to the window, but as he tried to prise hard on the trigger, the pistol swayed in his jittery grasp.

Bile rose in his throat, knowing his shots would only serve as a warning to the Outlaw, and his stance began to wilt. In that moment, the Outlaw turned to spring away from the window, and as he fleetingly paced across the yard, he shot a glance in Willis's direction and smiled.

Willis's eyes rounded wide with alarm and fear, and he reacted by submissively lowering his head and raising his forearms in front of his face in a cowardly but natural defence. Dropping his pistol, he closed his eyes and waited for the expected thunderous blast of lead to hurl him into the great unknown abyss, but instead, he was thankful when he heard only the fading patter of distant footsteps.

Expelling a lungful of relief, Willis wiped away the sweat of fear from his brow and stepped back into the darkness of the lean-to, not knowing if the Outlaw had seen him or not. He spat out the burning bile from within his throat, and his body trembled uncontrollably as the near-death experience washed over him.

Tillman looked up from his near-empty glass as approaching footsteps disturbed his pained recollections.

"What the hell do you want?" he growled at Willis before draining his glass.

Eduardo's place had emptied when the shots across the street at the Casa De Delicia had warned of danger, but Tillman, engrossed with the company of tequila, was too sullen to be intrigued, and he had remained seated at the bar with his head hung sluggishly low.

"She's all yours," Willis answered, tilting his head back and narrowing his eyes as he spoke, grim-faced.

"What?" Tillman slanted a suspicious glance towards Willis.

"You heard. I'm done with her and Mac's games."

"You mean you've finally realised Mac's gonna choose the better man?"

"Not quite… I've realised it's not Mac's choice."

"You jesting with me?"

Willis shrugged and remained silent as he noticed a huge smile on Tillman's face slowly stretch from ear to ear.

"I always knew it," he gloated. "And I'd often wonder when you'd finally ascertain you're not man enough for Liberty."

"I'm not a fool," Willis shook his head and spat. "That is—I'm not fool enough to stand in the way of the Outlaw."

Tillman's face flushed, and using the bar he elbowed himself up from his stool to tower over Willis.

"Outlaw!" He grabbed Willis by the throat with his left hand and pulled him close. "Outlaw… I think you better get to explaining yourself."

Tillman's eyes narrowed and his mouth tightened as he began to squeeze his grip around Willis's throat. "And be real quick about it before I crush your gullet."

"It's between you and him now. It's as I said, I'm done with Liberty," Willis conceded.

Tillman's grip strengthened, and his face shone purple. "What do you mean? Between me and him?" He pressed his forehead up to Willis's bulging eyes.

"I just happened to be checking in on Daisy at the Casa when I heard a loud ruckus inside," Willis screaked through his narrowed windpipe. "So I went down the side alley and into the rear yard where I saw Liberty canoodling with the Outlaw."

The choking increased. "I heard him promise to meet her later tonight over at Mac's place."

"And you didn't do anything, you cowardly son of a bitch?"

"I wasn't armed, and besides, I figured you'd want your chance to get even with him," he lied.

"And Dykes?"

"He's let him free, so I'm figuring you'd rid us of his bedevilment without placating the lawman."

"You gutless waster!" Tillman straightened out his arm, forcing Willis backwards. "Get out of my sight."

With the command, he pushed hard against Willis's throat, forcing him down to the sawdust-covered floor.

Then he pressed the flat of his foot hard against his backside to scurry him towards the door.

Tillman did not trust Willis and suspected a setup, but inflamed by alcohol and raged with jealousy, any caution was supplanted by misjudged confidence.

He stuck his teeth into the bandage on his right hand and bit hard to tear away the wrapping. Blood still dripped from the purple bullet hole in his hand. He stretched out his fingers and then clutched them into a tight ball. He cussed and screwed up his face as pain spasmed along his arm, but wild and bitter with alcohol venom, he repeated the act several times until, clenching his teeth, he could reach down with the bloodied hand and withdraw his pistol.

He held it by his waist for a few seconds until finally, ignoring the pain, he levelled the weapon to shoulder height. This time he cursed the Lord loudly and pulled the trigger repeatedly, firing several shots into the furthest beam.

"Gullible fool," Willis smiled to himself, hearing the shots in the distance as moonlight led him away from Eduardo's and towards West Valley ranch.

Tillman had baited him easily, just as he knew he would, and now all he had to do was wait in the thicket which surrounded the pasture and wait for his plan to unfurl.

Crouched in the darkness, clutching his Henry repeater rifle, he knew the Outlaw and Tillman would both be hidden in the shrubs waiting for Liberty to appear, and at the moment when the Outlaw showed himself to his darling he knew Tillman would also expose himself with blazing weapons to seek his retribution.

As the thunder and flame fired, from his position of advantage Willis planned to witness with relish the two gunmen unleashing their evil upon each other, and then just as silence was re-established he would execute the coup and claim the glory of killing the Outlaw, which would include Mac's gratification and consent for marriage.

Chapter 14

Liberty's fingers hurriedly feathered through the meagre contents of her dressing table drawer until they landed upon the only possession of her mother's which remained in the house: a large silver cast, turquoise and blue coral ring.

Carefully hidden away from Mac, it had escaped the mass bonfire of all Ruby May's possessions as a drunken, raged Mac tried to cure his mourning by collecting up and reducing to ashes all reminiscences of his young deceased wife.

On her return to the ranch, Liberty had saddled two of Mac's best horses and packed them heavily with supplies. Now she was ready to leave the bad memories and town which had never been her home behind her.

She turned towards the bedside lantern and angled her treasure to catch the light.

Liberty had been given the ring by her mother as her death rattle began to triumph, and understanding Mac, Liberty knew to hide away the keepsake, only daring to peek at its magnificence in the privacy of her room.

She sighed, looking at the ornate eagle which was set against the coral. She remembered her mother's words as she caringly placed the ring in her small palm and folded her dainty fingers around it to clasp it tight, knowing Mac's prying eyes were occupied somewhere else for a few moments.

"The eagle is the highest flying bird and is revered by the Caddo tribe because it flies near to their life's creator. The turquoise and blue coral represents the blood of your mother and the father sky. Cherish it well, my love."

At that point her mother's incessant sobbing slipped into a slurred and hushed apology because the ring was all she could bequeath to her daughter, and then, as short panting breaths set in, she begged her daughter to look after the keepsake so that she could pass it through the generations and preserve the memory of their heritage.

"Why the hell are you back?"

Mac's hollering from the open doorway startled her and she almost dropped the ring.

"Why aren't you whoring at the Casa?" He swayed, holding high a lantern which increased the deepness of his craggy age lines and the raggedness of his grey chin whiskers.

Fear caught in her throat, and numbness prevented an answer. She noticed his brow furrow as his eyes locked onto the glistening gold around her neck.

He recognised the jewellery, although he could not recall where from. He lipped the reflecting initials which were accentuated against her leather-coloured skin: "LM".

"What in the hell have you got there?"

"Nothing," she replied faintly. Then nervously she covered the gift with the flat of her hand, fidgeting with the ring in her fingers to prevent it falling to the floor.

Mac's eyes flickered between the ring and the necklace. "What in the hell?" His whiskey breath filled the room. "Where did you get those?"

He moved closer, his eyes flicking between her hand and the necklace he had seen before.

"Show me." He continued his forward stumbling gait, casting his mind back to years past. The fragrances of the bordello scented his nostrils and the smile of the previous madam momentarily distracted him.

"It's nothing of yours." Liberty twisted at her waist to shield her hand.

"Why you little squaw bitch!" He dropped his hand heavily on her shoulder and pulled her back to face him. "Everything in this house is mine."

The flat of his hand across her cheek followed the words, and the force of the violence thrust her onto the bed.

"You no good lousy bitch."

An instantaneous ear-piercing scream replaced the tirade, and it penetrated every room in the house as Liberty reached out and swooped upwards to smash the bedside lamp over Mac's head.

Darting sideways off the bed, she evaded the liquid flames which engulfed the hideous screaming man and fled the room.

In an agonised frenzy, Mac dropped his own lantern and began to manically slap the fierce flames which scorched his face and burned his hair. His own lamp crashed against the boards and another explosion flared up his body as a solid blaze engulfed him and splattered burning oil over the bed sheets.

Liberty glanced back over her shoulder as she fled the room and burnt flesh scorched her nostrils and smoke stung her eyes. She saw Mac's legs buckle beneath him and he writhed in the deadly furnace. He screamed for help, but with his frantic plea and draw of breath he only gulped in more lungfuls of flame and, sagging to the floor, he palpitated to a slow, torturous death.

Liberty continued her escape at pace along the hall and down the stairs, only pausing at the gun rack near the back porch. Grabbing a hold as she moved and cracking open Mac's rifle to check for bullets, Liberty burst through the rear door, dropped to her knees in the dirt, and gasped in lungfuls of the fresh night breeze.

From the seclusion of redbuds and willows, the Outlaw's face displayed concern as he saw the flicker of flame spread rapidly through the upstairs ranch window. Arising from one knee and taking half a step out onto the sloping pasture, he watched curiously as glass and flame exploded outwards.

With no sign of the girl, anxiety vexed and alarmed him. His pulse matched his increased breathing, and finally concern willed him to stride out into the open and run down the sloping wild grass towards the house.

Tillman's pulse raced, and he smiled when he saw the Outlaw step out from the darkness and rush down the pasture towards the burning house. The killer had been hidden only twenty yards higher on the slope than the militia man, and racing towards the house, he was now almost parallel.

Tillman did not need to unholster his pistol. He had been impatiently waiting to discharge his slaughter, and so he was set and ready. Leaning forward to fix his aim, an evil smirk stretched across his face as he watched the Outlaw ease his stride to a near halt and present himself as a perfect target. Tillman glanced beyond his aim to see the distant silhouette of Liberty May dashing towards the pasture to meet the Outlaw in the glow of the flames.

With his eyes and thoughts focused entirely on Liberty May, the Outlaw did not hear the creek of Tillman's hammer, but the flash and sounding eruption of lead to his side caused him to instinctively reach down for his pistol.

Hundreds of night birds screamed and flapped in a panicked escape from the trees as the blast of lead disturbed their solace, leaving the branches to sway as if a sudden gust had caught them.

Intense, bolting pain in his chest thrust the Outlaw sideways and, losing all coordination, he stumbled backwards and dropped to the mud with his gun in his hand.

In the distance, a faint scream reached Tillman's ears and he angled his head towards Liberty, whose deflated dark figure against the raging inferno denoted her testimony to the shooting.

From the higher ground of the pasture, Willis had also curiously watched the fire ravage Mac's homestead, then gleefully observed the Outlaw's demise by the flash of the concealed assassin. Self-satisfaction swooped over him, and a gutless demonic spirit roused his courage to finish the deceit. Keeping his head low, he dishonourably scurried through the dense bark to encircle the gunmen.

"Thought you'd humiliate me," Tillman scorned and baited the pained man. "End my days as a cripple."

The Outlaw's senses were scrambled, and his vision blurred. He panted rapidly, trying to fill his lungs and regain his breath. He could not hear the words of the approaching gunman, but his failing consciousness recognised he had been ambushed and his life was in jeopardy.

The blackness of the night and the orange of the distant flames conquered all clarity, and he repeatedly clasped his eyelids tight and reopened them to try and clear his vision and hold still the spinning figure who approached.

"Not so fearsome now, are you?"

Believing himself in full control and safe, Tillman switched his gun into his left hand to relieve the throbbing wound, and wincing, he stretched out his fingers to shake away the dripping blood.

The Outlaw clamped hard on his teeth and braced himself. Now he recognised the blurred man's accent.

"Just a mortal with a gun that bleeds like the rest of us." Tillman's eyes remained fixed on the heavily panting target. "Brought to justice by Charles Tillman. Hero of Rio Rojo, La Vaca County." The thought pleased him. "That's what they'll print in the Tribune come sunup."

He switched the shooter back into his right hand and directed it at the Outlaw. "Shame you won't be around to read it."

Tillman flexed his fingers and wrapped them tight again around his pistol, then he grinned as he pulled hard on the trigger.

An explosion erupted and a brief flash behind Tillman illuminated Willis as he emerged from the trees with his smoking gun.

Tillman's eyes bulged wide as a deep burn drilled straight through him. He dropped his gun to the grassy mud and staggered two steps before falling to his knees.

He tried to yell as he twisted his head sideways, but only blood and spittle were emitted.

Then, blinking water from his eyes, he scanned across the incandescent semi-darkness at the gunman.

Two more quick blasts from the darkness hurled Tillman's lifeless body to the dirt and thrust his soul to death's summons.

The Outlaw summoned all his strength and stretched out his fingers towards his gun, but he could only brush the oak handle as the pain in his chest caused him to retract his arm quickly and forced him to press his palm over the blood-seeping wound.

"Afraid your time's up too, Outlaw," warned Willis as he strode with the purpose of completing the slaughter. "The abode of the dead waits for you."

"No, wait!" Liberty May's dark outline stepped into the umber cast of the burning house. "Don't shoot," she cried.

"Ah, Libby, just in time to witness my glory." Willis fixed his aim and sneered.

Liberty angled herself sideward and began to raise Mac's rifle towards Willis.

"I know full well you can't shoot," he derided with a leer of nonchalance. "So drop the pretence."

He beckoned her with his hand. "Come over here and stand by my side as I send this murdering son of a bitch to hell."

Determined to either live her life with the man who briefly touched her heart or die beside him, Liberty defied Willis and levelled the rifle at him.

Willis focused his eyes along his outstretched arm and took aim at the maimed man, but a glint reflecting from the light of the orange flames stole his attention.

His eyes flickered from the wounded man to the shimmering necklace set against Liberty's dark skin. His forehead furrowed, his eyes narrowed, and his face told a knowing story as he recognised the unique necklace which was bejewelled with the initials "LM".

"What... where... did..."

A blast of lead from the direction of the floor immediately ceased Willis' speculation as a bullet from the Outlaw's gun bore deep into his forehead. Willis swayed briefly, his blank eyes still fixed on the neck ornament, his face void of all vitality. Slowly his arm lowered and hung loose. He staggered sideways and his numb fingers released his gun to the floor, then he dropped face-forward with an uncontrolled thud.

From the violence fell a palette of peacefulness and a surreal stillness, which was only interrupted by the crackle of burning wood in the distance.

Liberty dropped the rifle and rushed through the thick gunpowder smoke to kneel at the Outlaw's side.

A smile cast aside his pained frown, and he dropped the Tranter so he could meet her reaching hand.

"You came."

"You doubted me." He raised his shoulder from the floor and his face met her lips.

Until that moment when their lips met, he did not know if she was real or if a holy apparition had come to guide him from Earth.

"Never." She broke the kiss momentarily to answer.

"And now…" He pulled his head back slightly. Her perfume had replaced the gun smoke in his nostrils.

"Now we are together." She gripped tight his hand and snugged it into her bosom to hold it tight.

"Maybe not for so long." The Outlaw brushed his fingers over the hole in his waistcoat and looked at the poppy-coloured liquid that flowed and tainted his skin.

"You left me once and you sure in hell ain't ever going to leave me again."

Liberty carefully tugged his leather vest and prised open his black wet shirt to inspect the blood-pumping hole. Then she slid her palm around his back to feel for more blood; only dust was found.

"The bullet is stuck in a bone. We need to find a doctor," she confirmed, tearing squarely a piece of her petticoat and folding it neatly to press on the open wound.

"Your love will heal me." He noted the welling in her eyes, and he brushed a teardrop from her cheek with his thumb. "Your love can make me survive anything."

"Hold this real tight and don't let it move." She took his hand from her face and applied it firmly over the padded cloth, then she placed her shoulder under his arm to haul him to his feet.

The vibrant pastel hue of the fire cast a huge shadow of their coupled bodies over the now serene field of death.

"Look at your home," the Outlaw said, tilting his face away from the sky-reaching glow.

"It was never my home," Liberty said, holding him steady.

The fire snapped behind them.

"Where do you want to go?" he asked.

Liberty didn't look at the burning ranch.

"Anywhere we can't be followed."

He studied her for a long moment.

"We? Do you trust me?"

She nodded, her smile landing heavier than certainty.

He exhaled slowly.

"Then stay close."

"Always."

They moved together into the dark.

"We won't ever be safe."

"No... but we'll be free, far away and togther."

He tightened his grip on her hand and they didn't look back.

Other Westerns by Daniel Carlson include;

The Apostle

The Badge and the Bullet

The Vengeance Trail

The Return

Life Taker - The Story of the Gun

The Life and Death of My Best Friend, Davy Crockett

The Betryal